CATTLE BRANDS

CATTLE BRANDS

A Collection of Western Camp-Fire Stories

BY

ANDY ADAMS

Short Story Index Reprint Series

 BOOKS FOR LIBRARIES PRESS
FREEPORT, NEW YORK

First Published 1934
Reprinted 1971

INTERNATIONAL STANDARD BOOK NUMBER:
0-8369-3831-3

LIBRARY OF CONGRESS CATALOG CARD NUMBER:
70-150534

PRINTED IN THE UNITED STATES OF AMERICA

TO

MR. AND MRS. HENRY RUSSELL WRAY

CONTENTS

BRANDS

Brand	Description	Brand	Description
— X —	Bar X bar.	O O O	Three circle.
OIO	Ohio.	=	Two bars.
┿┿┿	Barb wire.	↘↗	Broken arrow.
⌐╹⌐	Hat.	4 D	Four D.
⌀	Apple.	⊀	Turkey track.
◆〜〜	Diamond tail.	— B Q.	Owned by "Barbecue" Campbell.
IOA	Iowa.	X	L. X.
J + H	Johnson & Hosmer.	I. C.	"Inspected and condemned." [1]
U. S.	United States. [1]	⊥⊽	Spade.
S.	"Sold." [1]	⚘	Flower pot.
⚲	Dead tree.	⟋	Frying pan.
⊏⊐	Tin cup.	⚘	Laurel leaf.
ɑ〜〜	Snake.	X — 2	X bar two.
— Z —	Bar Z bar.		
∿	Running W.		

[1] These three belong to the United States Government.

CATTLE BRANDS

I

DRIFTING NORTH

IT was a wet, bad year on the Old Western Trail. From Red River north and all along was herd after herd waterbound by high water in the rivers. Our outfit lay over nearly a week on the South Canadian, but we were not alone, for there were five other herds waiting for the river to go down. This river had tumbled over her banks for several days, and the driftwood that was coming down would have made it dangerous swimming for cattle.

We were expected to arrive in Dodge early in June, but when we reached the North Fork of the Canadian, we were two weeks behind time.

Old George Carter, the owner of the herd, was growing very impatient about us, for he had had no word from us after we had crossed Red River at Doan's crossing. Other cowmen lying around Dodge, who had herds on the trail, could hear nothing from their men, but in their experience and confidence in their

outfits guessed the cause — it was water. Our
surprise when we came opposite Camp Supply
to have Carter and a stranger ride out to meet
us was not to be measured. They had got impatient waiting, and had taken the mail buckboard to Supply, making inquiries along the
route for the *Hat* herd, which had not passed
up the trail, so they were assured. Carter was
so impatient that he could not wait, as he had
a prospective buyer on his hands, and the delay in the appearing of the herd was very an-
noying to him. Old George was as tickled as
a little boy to meet us all.

The cattle were looking as fine as silk. The
lay-overs had rested them. The horses were
in good trim, considering the amount of wet
weather we had had. Here and there was a
nigger brand, but these saddle galls were unavoidable when using wet blankets. The cattle were twos and threes. We had left western
Texas with a few over thirty-two hundred
head and were none shy. We could have
counted out more, but on some of them the
Hat brand had possibly faded out. We went
into a cosy camp early in the evening. Everything needful was at hand, wood, water, and
grass. Cowmen in those days prided themselves on their outfits, and Carter was a trifle
gone on his men.

With the cattle on hand, drinking was out of the question, so the only way to show us any regard was to bring us a box of cigars. He must have brought those cigars from Texas, for they were wrapped in a copy of the Fort Worth "Gazette." It was a month old and full of news. Every man in the outfit read and reread it. There were several train robberies reported in it, but that was common in those days. They had nominated for Governor "The Little Cavalryman," Sol Ross, and this paper estimated that his majority would be at least two hundred thousand. We were all anxious to get home in time to vote for him.

Theodore Baughman was foreman of our outfit. Baugh was a typical trail-boss. He had learned to take things as they came, play the cards as they fell, and not fret himself about little things that could not be helped. If we had been a month behind he would never have thought to explain the why or wherefore to old man Carter. Several years after this, when he was scouting for the army, he rode up to a herd over on the Chisholm trail and asked one of the tail men: "Son, have you seen anything of about three hundred nigger soldiers?" "No," said the cowboy. "Well," said Baugh, "I've lost about that many."

That night around camp the smoke was curling upward from those cigars in clouds. When supper was over and the guards arranged for the night, story-telling was in order. This cattle-buyer with us lived in Kansas City and gave us several good ones. He told us of an attempted robbery of a bank which had occurred a few days before in a western town. As a prelude to the tale, he gave us the history of the robbers.

"Cow Springs, Kansas," said he, "earned the reputation honestly of being a hard cow-town. When it became the terminus of one of the many eastern trails, it was at its worst. The death-rate amongst its city marshals — always due to a six-shooter in the hands of some man who never hesitated to use it — made the office not over desirable. The office was vacated so frequently in this manner that at last no local man could be found who would have it. Then the city fathers sent to Texas for a man who had the reputation of being a killer. He kept his record a vivid green by shooting first and asking questions afterward.

"Well, the first few months he filled the office of marshal he killed two white men and an Indian, and had the people thoroughly buffaloed. When the cattle season had ended and winter came on, the little town grew tame and listless. There was no man to dare him to shoot, and he longed for other worlds to conquer. He had won his way into public confidence with his little gun. But this confidence reposed in him was misplaced, for he proved his own double both in morals and courage.

"To show you the limit of the confidence he enjoyed: the treasurer of the Cherokee Strip Cattle Association paid rent money to that tribe, at their capital, fifty thousand dollars quarterly. The capital is not located on any railroad; so the funds in currency were taken in regularly by the treasurer, and turned over to the tribal authorities. This trip was always made with secrecy, and the marshal was taken along as a trusted guard. It was an extremely dangerous trip to make, as it was through a country infested with robbers and the capital at least a hundred miles from the railroad. Strange no one ever attempted to rob the stage or private conveyance, though this sum was taken in regularly for several years. The average robber was careful of his person, and could not be induced to make a target of himself for any money consideration, where there was danger of a gun in the hands of a man that would shoot rapidly and carelessly.

"Before the herds began to reach as far north, the marshal and his deputy gave some excuse and disappeared for a few days, which was quite common and caused no comment. One fine morning the good people of the town where the robbery was attempted were thrown into an uproar by shooting in their bank, just at the opening hour. The robbers were none other than our trusted marshal, his deputy, and a cow-puncher who had been led into the deal. When they ordered the officials of the bank to stand in a row with hands up, they were nonplused at their refusal to comply. The attacked party unearthed ugly looking guns and opened fire on the hold-ups instead.

"This proved bad policy, for when the smoke cleared away the cashier, a very popular man, was found dead, while an assistant was dangerously wounded. The shooting, however, had aroused the town to the situation, and men were seen running to and fro with guns. This unexpected refusal and the consequent shooting spoiled the plans of the robbers, so that they abandoned the robbery and ran to their horses.

"After mounting they parleyed with each other a moment and seemed bewildered as to which way they should ride, finally riding south toward what seemed a broken country. Very few minutes elapsed before every man who could find a horse was joining the posse that was forming to pursue them. Before they were out of sight the posse had started after them. They were well mounted and as determined a set of men as were ever called upon to meet a similar emergency. They had the decided advantage of the robbers, as their horses were fresh, and the men knew every foot of the country.

"The broken country to which the hold-ups headed was a delusion as far as safety was concerned. They were never for a moment out of sight of the pursuers, and this broken country ended in a deep coulee. When the posse saw them enter this they knew that their capture was only a matter of time. Nature seemed against the robbers, for as they entered the coulee their horses bogged down in a springy rivulet, and they were so hard pressed that they hastily dismounted, and sought shelter in some shrubbery that grew about. The pursuing party, now swollen to quite a number, had spread out and by this time surrounded the men. They were seen to take shelter in a clump of wild plum brush, and the posse closed in on them. Seeing the numbers against them, they came out on demand and surrendered. Neither the posse nor themselves knew at this time that the shooting in the bank had killed the cashier. Less than an hour's time had elapsed between the shooting and the capture. When the posse reached town on their return, they learned of the death of the cashier, and the identity of the prisoners was soon established by citizens who knew the marshal and his deputy. The latter admitted their identity.

"That afternoon they were photographed, and later in the day were given a chance to write to any friends to whom they wished to say good-by. The cow-puncher was the only one who availed himself of the opportunity. He wrote to his parents. He was the only one of the trio who had the nerve to write, and seemed the only one who realized the enormity of his crime, and that he would never see the sun of another day.

"As darkness settled over the town, the mob assembled. There was no demonstration. The men were taken quietly out and hanged. At the final moment there was a remarkable variety of nerve shown. The marshal and deputy were limp, unable to stand on their feet. With piteous appeals and tears they pleaded for mercy, something they themselves had never shown their own victims. The boy who had that day written his parents his last letter met his fate with Indian stoicism. He cursed the crouching figures of his pardners for enticing him into this crime, and begged them not to die like curs, but to meet bravely the fate which he admitted they all deserved. Several of the men in the mob came forward and shook hands with him, and with no appeal to man or his Maker, he was swung into the great Unknown at the end of a rope. Such nerve is seldom met in life, and those that are supposed to have it, when they come face to face with their end, are found lacking that quality. It is a common anomaly in life that the bad man with his record often shows the white feather when he meets his fate at the hands of an outraged community."

We all took a friendly liking to the cattle-buyer. He was an interesting talker. While he was a city man, he mixed with us with a certain freedom and abandon that was easy and natural. We all regretted it the next day when he and the old man left us.

"I've heard my father tell about those Cherokees," said Port Cole. "They used to live in Georgia, those Indians. They must have been honest people, for my father told us boys at home, that once in the old State while the Cherokees lived there, his father hired one of their tribe to guide him over the mountains. There was a pass through the mountains that was used and known only to these Indians. It would take six weeks to go and come, and to attend to the business in view. My father was a small boy at the time, and says that his father hired the guide for the entire trip for forty dollars in gold. One condition was that the money was to be paid in advance. The morning was set for the start, and my grandfather took my father along on the trip.

"Before starting from the Indian's cabin my grandfather took out his purse and paid the Indian four ten-dollar gold pieces. The Indian walked over to the corner of the cabin, and in the presence of other Indians laid this gold, in plain sight of all, on the end of a log that projected where they cross outside, and got on his horse to be gone six weeks. They made the trip on time, and my father said his first thought, on their return to the Indian village, was to see if the money was untouched. It was. You could n't risk white folks that way."

"Oh, I don't know," said one of the boys. "Suppose you save your wages this summer and try it next year when we start up the trail, just to see how it will work."

"Well, if it 's just the same to you," replied Port, lighting a fresh cigar, "I 'll not try, for I 'm well enough satisfied as to how it would turn out, without testing it."

"Is n't it strange," said Bat Shaw, "that if you trust a man or put confidence in him he won't betray you. Now, that marshal — one month he was guarding money at the risk of his life, and the next was losing his life trying to rob some one. I remember a similar case down on the Rio Grande. It was during the boom in sheep a few years ago, when every one got crazy over sheep.

"A couple of Americans came down on the river to buy sheep. They brought their money with them. It was before the time of any railroads. The man they deposited their money with had lived amongst these Mexicans till he had forgotten where he did belong, though he was a Yankee. These sheep-buyers asked their banker to get them a man who spoke Spanish and knew the country, as a guide. The banker sent and got a man that he could trust. He was a swarthy-looking native whose appearance would not recommend him anywhere. He was accepted, and they set out to be gone over a month.

"They bought a band of sheep, and it was necessary to pay for them at a point some forty miles further up the river. There had been some robbing along the river, and these men felt uneasy about carrying the money to this place to pay for the sheep. The banker came to the rescue by advising them to send the money by the Mexican, who could take it through in a single night. No one would ever suspect him of ever having a dollar on his person. It looked risky, but the banker who knew the nature of the native urged it as the better way, assuring them that the Mexican was perfectly trustworthy. The peon was brought in, the situation was explained to him, and he was ordered to be in readiness at night-fall to start on his errand.

"He carried the money over forty miles that night, and delivered it safely in the morning to the proper parties. This act of his aroused the admiration of these sheep men beyond a point of safety. They paid for the sheep, were gone for a few months, sold out their flocks to good advantage, and came back to buy more. This second time they did not take the precaution to have the banker hire the man, but did so themselves, intending to deposit their money with a different house farther up the river. They confided to him that they had quite a sum of money with them, and that they would deposit it with the same merchant to whom he had carried the money before. The first night they camped the Mexican murdered them both, took the money, and crossed into Mexico. He hid their bodies, and it was months before they were missed, and a year before their bones were found. He had plenty of time to go to the ends of the earth before his crime would be discovered.

"Now that Mexican would never think of betraying the banker, his old friend and patron, his *muy bueno amigo*. There were obligations that he could not think of breaking with the banker; but these fool sheep men, supposing it was simple honesty, paid the penalty of their confidence with their lives. Now, when he rode over this same road alone, a few months before, with over five thousand dollars in money belonging to these same men, all he would need to have done was to ride across the river. When there were no obligations binding, he was willing to add murder to robbery. Some folks say that Mexicans are good people; it is the climate, possibly, but they can always be depended on to assay high in treachery."

"What guard are you going to put me on to-night?" inquired old man Carter of Baugh.

"This outfit," said Baugh, in reply, "don't allow any tenderfoot around the cattle, — at night, at least. You'd better play you're company; somebody that's come. If you're so very anxious to do something, the cook may let you rustle wood or carry water. We'll fix you up a bed after a little, and see that you get into it where you can sleep and be harmless.

"Colonel," added Baugh, "why is it that you never tell that experience you had once amongst the greasers?"

"Well, there was nothing funny in it to me," said Carter, "and they say I never tell it twice alike."

"Why, certainly, tell us," said the cattlebuyer. "I've never heard it. Don't throw off to-night."

"It was a good many years ago," began old man George, "but the incident is very clear in my mind. I was working for a month's wages then myself. We were driving cattle out of Mexico. The people I was working for contracted for a herd down in Chihuahua, about four hundred miles south of El Paso. We sent in our own outfit, wagon, horses, and men, two weeks before. I was kept behind to take in the funds to pay for the cattle. The day before I started, my people drew out of the bank twenty-eight thousand dollars, mostly large bills. They wired ahead and engaged a rig to take me from the station where I left the railroad to the ranch, something like ninety miles.

"I remember I bought a new mole-skin suit, which was very popular about then. I had nothing but a small hand-bag, and it contained only a six-shooter. I bought a book to read on the train and on the road out, called 'Other People's Money.' The title caught my fancy, and it was very interesting. It was written by a Frenchman, — full of love and thrilling situations. I had the money belted on me securely, and started out with flying colors. The railroad runs through a dreary country, not worth a second look, so I read my new book. When I arrived at the station I found the conveyance awaiting me. The plan was to drive halfway, and stay over night at a certain hacienda.

"The driver insisted on starting at once, telling me that we could reach the Hacienda Grande by ten o'clock that night, which would be half my journey. We had a double-seated buckboard and covered the country rapidly. There were two Mexicans on the front seat, while I had the rear one all to myself. Once on the road I interested myself in 'Other People's Money,' almost forgetful of the fact that at that very time I had enough of other people's money on my person to set all the bandits in Mexico on my trail. There was nothing of incident that evening, until an hour before sundown. We reached a small ranchito, where we spent an hour changing horses, had coffee and a rather light lunch.

"Before leaving I noticed a Pinto horse hitched to a tree some distance in the rear of the house, and as we were expecting to buy a number of horses, I walked back and looked this one carefully over. He was very peculiarly color-marked in the mane. I inquired for his owner, but they told me that he was not about at present. It was growing dusk when we started out again. The evening was warm and sultry and threatening rain. We had been on our way about an hour when I realized we had left the main road and were bumping along on a by-road. I asked the driver his reason for this, and he explained that it was a cut-off, and that by taking it we would save three miles and half an hour's time. As a further reason he expressed his opinion that we would have rain that night, and that he was anxious to reach the hacienda in good time. I encouraged him to drive faster, which he did. Within another hour I noticed we were going down a dry arroyo, with mesquite brush on both sides of the road, which was little better than a trail. My suspicions were never aroused sufficiently to open the little hand-bag and belt on the six-shooter. I was dreaming along when we came to a sudden stop before what seemed a deserted jacal. The Mexicans mumbled something to each other over some disappointment, when the driver said to me: —

"'Here's where we stay all night. This is the hacienda.' They both got out and insisted on my getting out, but I refused to do so. I reached down and picked up my little grip and was in the act of opening it, when one of them grabbed my arm and jerked me out of the seat to the ground. I realized then for the first time that I was in for it in earnest. I never knew before that I could put up such a fine defense, for inside a minute I had them both blinded in their own blood. I gathered up rocks and had them flying when I heard a clatter of hoofs coming down the arroyo like a squadron of cavalry. They were so close on to me that I took to the brush, without hat, coat, or pistol. Men that pack a gun all their lives never have it when they need it; that was exactly my fix. Darkness was in my favor, but I had no more idea where I was or which way I was going than a baby. One thing sure, I was trying to get away from there as fast as I could. The night was terribly dark, and about ten o'clock it began to rain a deluge. I kept going all night, but must have been circling.

"Towards morning I came to an arroyo which was running full of water. My idea was to get that between me and the scene of my trouble, so I took off my boots to wade it. When about one third way across, I either stepped off a bluff bank or into a well, for I went under and dropped the boots. When I came to the surface I made a few strokes swimming and landed in a clump of mesquite brush, to which I clung, got on my feet, and waded out to the opposite bank more scared than hurt. Right there I lay until daybreak.

"The thing that I remember best now was the peculiar odor of the wet mole-skin. If there had been a strolling artist about looking for a picture of Despair, I certainly would have filled the bill. The sleeves were torn out of my shirt, and my face and arms were scratched and bleeding from the thorns of the mesquite. No one who could have seen me then would ever have dreamed that I was a walking depositary of 'Other People's Money.' When it got good daylight I started out and kept the shelter of the brush to hide me. After nearly an hour's travel, I came out on a divide, and about a mile off I saw what looked like a jacal. Directly I noticed a smoke arise, and I knew then it was a habitation. My appearance was not what I desired, but I approached it.

"In answer to my knock at the door a woman opened it about two inches and seemed to be more interested in examination of my anatomy than in listening to my troubles. After I had made an earnest sincere talk she asked me, 'No estay loco tu ?' I assured her that I was perfectly sane, and that all I needed was food and clothing, for which I would pay her well. It must have been my appearance that aroused her sympathy, for she admitted me and fed me.

"The woman had a little girl of probably ten years of age. This little girl brought me water to wash myself, while the mother prepared me something to eat. I was so anxious to pay these people that I found a five-dollar gold piece in one of my pockets and gave it to the little girl, who in turn gave it to her mother. While I was drinking the coffee and eating my breakfast, the woman saw me looking at a picture of the Virgin Mary which was hanging on the adobe wall opposite me. She asked me if I was a Catholic, which I admitted. Then she brought out a shirt and offered it to me.

"Suddenly the barking of a dog attracted her to the door. She returned breathless, and said in good Spanish: 'For God's sake, run! Fly! Don't let my husband and brother catch you here, for they are coming home.' She thrust the shirt into my hand and pointed out the direction in which I should go. From a concealed point of the brush I saw two men ride up to the jacal and dismount. One of them was riding the Pinto horse I had seen the day before.

"I kept the brush for an hour or so, and finally came out on the mesa. Here I found a flock of sheep and a pastore. From this shepherd I learned that I was about ten miles from the main road. He took the sandals from his own feet and fastened them on mine, gave me directions, and about night I reached the hacienda, where I was kindly received and cared for. This ranchero sent after officers and had the country scoured for the robbers. I was detained nearly a week, to see if I could identify my drivers, without result. They even brought in the owner of the Pinto horse, and no doubt husband of the woman who saved my life.

" After a week's time I joined our own outfit, and I never heard a language that sounded so sweet as the English of my own tongue. I would have gone back and testified against the owner of the spotted horse if it had n't been for a woman and a little girl who depended on him, robber that he was."

"Now, girls," said Baugh, addressing Carter and the stranger, "I've made you a bed out of the wagon-sheet, and rustled a few blankets from the boys. You'll find the bed under the wagon-tongue, and we've stretched a fly over it to keep the dew off you, besides adding privacy to your apartments. So you can turn in when you run out of stories or get sleepy."

"Have n't you got one for us?" inquired the cattle-buyer of Baugh. "This is no time to throw off, or refuse to be sociable."

"Well, now, that bank robbery that you were telling the boys about," said Baugh, as he bit the tip from a fresh cigar, "reminds me of a hold-up that I was in up in the San Juan mining country in Colorado. We had driven into that mining camp a small bunch of beef and had sold them to fine advantage. The outfit had gone back, and I remained behind to collect for the cattle, expecting to take the stage and overtake the outfit down on the river. I had neglected to book my passage in advance, so when the stage was ready to start I had to content myself with a seat on top. I don't remember the amount of money I had. It was the proceeds of something like one hundred and fifty beeves, in a small bag along of some old clothes. There was n't a cent of it mine, still I was supposed to look after it.

"The driver answered to the name of South-Paw, drove six horses, and we had a jolly crowd on top. Near midnight we were swinging along, and as we rounded a turn in the road, we noticed a flickering light ahead some distance which looked like the embers of a camp-fire. As we came nearly opposite the light, the leaders shied at some object in the road in front of them. South-Paw uncurled his whip, and was in the act of pouring the leather into them, when that light was uncovered as big as the head-light of an engine. An empty five-gallon oil-can had been cut in half and used as a reflector, throwing full light into the road sufficient to cover the entire coach. Then came a round of orders which meant business. 'Shoot them leaders if they cross that obstruction!' 'Kill any one that gets off on the opposite side!' 'Driver, move up a few feet farther!' 'A few feet farther, please.' 'That'll do; thank you, sir.' 'Now, every son-of-a-horse-thief, get out on this side of the coach, please, and be quick about it!'

"The man giving these orders stood a few feet behind the lamp and out of sight, but the muzzle of a Winchester was plainly visible and seemed to cover every man on the stage. It is needless to say that we obeyed, got down in the full glare of the light, and lined up with our backs to the robber, hands in the air. There was a heavily veiled woman on the stage, whom he begged to hold the light for him, assuring her that he never robbed a woman. This veiled person disappeared at the time, and was supposed to have been a confederate. When the light was held for him, he drew a black cap over each one of us, searching everybody for weapons. Then he proceeded to rob us, and at last went through the mail. It took him over an hour to do the job; he seemed in no hurry.

"It was not known what he got out of the mail, but the passengers yielded about nine hundred revenue to him, while there was three times that amount on top the coach in my grip, wrapped in a dirty flannel shirt. When he disappeared we were the cheapest lot of men imaginable. It was amusing to hear the excuses, threats, and the like; but the fact remained the same, that a dozen of us had been robbed by a lone highwayman. I felt good over it, as the money in the grip had been overlooked.

" Well, we cleared out the obstruction in the road, and got aboard the coach once more. About four o'clock in the morning we arrived at our destination, only two hours late. In the hotel office where the stage stopped was the very man who had robbed us. He had got in an hour ahead of us, and was a very much interested listener to the incident as retold. There was an early train out of town that morning, and at a place where they stopped for breakfast he sat at the table with several drummers who were in the hold-up, a most attentive listener.

"He was captured the same day. He had hired a horse out of a livery stable the day before, to ride out to look at a ranch he thought of buying. The liveryman noticed that he limped slightly. He had collided with lead in Texas, as was learned afterward. The horse which had been hired to the ranch-buyer of the day before was returned to the corral of the livery barn at an unknown hour during the night, and suspicion settled on the lame man. When he got off the train at Pueblo, he walked into the arms of officers. The limp had marked him clearly.

"In a grip which he carried were a number of sacks, which he supposed contained gold dust, but held only taulk on its way to assayers in Denver. These he had gotten out of the express the night before, supposing they were valuable. We were all detained as witnesses. He was tried for robbing the mails, and was the coolest man in the court room. He was a tall, awkward-looking fellow, light complexioned, with a mild blue eye. His voice, when not disguised, would mark him amongst a thousand men. It was peculiarly mild and soft, and would lure a babe from its mother's arms.

"At the trial he never tried to hide his past, and you could n't help liking the fellow for his frank answers.

"'Were you ever charged with any crime before?' asked the prosecution. 'If so, when and where?'

"'Yes,' said the prisoner, 'in Texas, for robbing the mails in '77.'

"'What was the result?' continued the prosecution.

"'They sent me over the road for ninety-nine years.'

"'Then how does it come that you are at liberty?' quizzed the attorney.

"'Well, you see the President of the United States at that time was a warm personal friend of mine, though we had drifted apart somewhat. When he learned that the Federal authorities had interfered with my liberties, he pardoned me out instantly.'

"'What did you do then?' asked the attorney.

" 'Well, I went back to Texas, and was attending to my own business, when I got into a little trouble and had to kill a man. Lawyers down there won't do anything for you without you have money, and as I did n't have any for them, I came up to this country to try and make an honest dollar.'

" He went over the road a second time, and was n't in the Federal prison a year before he was released through influence. Prison walls were never made to hold as cool a rascal as he was. Have you a match? "

It was an ideal night. Millions of stars flecked the sky overhead. No one seemed willing to sleep. We had heard the evening gun and the trumpets sounding tattoo over at the fort, but their warnings of the closing day were not for us. The guards changed, the cattle sleeping like babes in a trundle-bed. Finally one by one the boys sought their blankets, while sleep and night wrapped these children of the plains in her arms.

II

SEIGERMAN'S PER CENT

TOWARDS the wind-up of the Cherokee Strip Cattle Association it became hard to ride a chuck-line in winter. Some of the cattle companies on the range, whose headquarters were far removed from the scene of active operations, saw fit to give orders that the common custom of feeding all comers and letting them wear their own welcome out must be stopped. This was hard on those that kept open house the year round. There was always a surplus of men on the range in the winter. Sometimes there might be ten men at a camp, and only two on the payroll. These extra men were called "chuckline riders." Probably eight months in the year they all had employment. At many camps they were welcome, as they would turn to and help do anything that was wanted done.

After a hard freeze it would be necessary to cut the ice, so that the cattle could water. A reasonable number of guests were no drawback at a time like this, as the chuck-line men would be the most active in opening the ice with axes. The cattle belonging to those who kept open house never got so far away that some one did n't recognize the brand and turn them back towards their own pasture. It was possible to cast bread upon the waters, even on the range.

The new order of things was received with many protests. Late in the fall three worthies of the range formed a combine, and laid careful plans of action, in case they should get let out of a winter's job. "I 've been on the range a good while," said Baugh, the leader of this trio, "but hereafter I 'll not ride my horses down, turning back the brand of any hidebound cattle company."

" That won't save you from getting hit with a cheque for your time when the snow begins to drift," commented Stubb.

" When we make our grand tour of the State this winter," remarked Arab Ab, "we 'll get that cheque of Baugh's cashed, together with our own. One thing sure, we won't fret about it; still we might think that riding a chuckline would beat footing it in a granger country, broke."

"Oh, we won't go broke," said Baugh, who was the leader in the idea that they would go to Kansas for the winter, and come back in the spring when men are wanted.

So when the beef season had ended, the calves had all been branded up and everything made snug for the winter, the foreman said to the boys at breakfast one morning, "Well, lads, I've kept you on the pay-roll as long as there has been anything to do, but this morning I'll have to give you your time. These recent orders of mine are sweeping, for they cut me down to one man, and we are to do our own cooking. I'm sorry that any of you that care to can't spend the winter with us. It's there that my orders are very distasteful to me, for I know what it is to ride a chuck-line myself. You all know that it's no waste of affection by this company that keeps even two of us on the pay-roll."

While the foreman was looking up accounts and making out the time of each, Baugh asked him, "When is the wagon going in after the winter's supplies?"

"In a day or two," answered the foreman. "Why?"

"Why, Stubby, Arab, and myself want to leave our saddles and private horses here with you until spring. We're going up in the State for the winter, and will wait and go in with the wagon."

"That will be all right," said the foreman. "You'll find things right side up when you come after them, and a job if I can give it to you."

"Don't you think it's poor policy," asked Stubb of the foreman, as the latter handed him his time, "to refuse the men a roof and the bite they eat in winter?"

"You may ask that question at headquarters, when you get your time cheque cashed. I've learned not to think contrary to my employers; not in the mouth of winter, anyhow."

"Oh, we don't care," said Baugh; "we're going to take in the State for a change of scenery. We'll have a good time and plenty of fun on the side."

The first snow-squall of the season came that night, and the wagon could not go in for several days. When the weather moderated the three bade the foreman a hearty good-by and boarded the wagon for town, forty miles away. This little village was a supply point for the range country to the south, and lacked that diversity of entertainment that the trio desired. So to a larger town westward, a county seat, they hastened by rail. This hamlet they took in by sections. There were the games running to suit their tastes, the variety theatre with its painted girls, and handbills announced that on the 24th of December and Christmas Day there would be horse races.

To do justice to all this melted their money fast.

Their gay round of pleasure had no check until the last day of the races. Heretofore they had held their own in the games, and the first day of the races they had even picked several winners. But grief was in store for Baugh the leader, Baugh the brains of the trio. He had named the winners so easily the day before, that now his confidence knew no bounds. His opinion was supreme on a running horse, though he cautioned the others not to risk their judgment — in fact, they had better follow him. "I'm going to back that sorrel gelding, that won yesterday, in the free-for-all to-day," said he to Stubb and Arab, "and if you boys go in with me, we'll make a killing."

"You can lose your money on a horse race too quick to suit me," replied Stubb. "I prefer to stick to poker; but you go ahead and win all you can, for spring is a long ways off yet."

"My observation of you as a poker player, my dear Stubby, is that you generally play the first hand to win and all the rest to get even."

They used up considerable time scoring for the free-for-all running race Christmas Day, during which delay Baugh not only got all his money bet, but his watch and a new overcoat.

The race went off with the usual dash, when there were no more bets in sight ; and when it ended Baugh buttoned up the top button of his coat, pulled his hat down over his eyes, and walked back from the race track in a meditative state of mind, to meet Stubb and Arab Ab.

"When I gamble and lose I never howl," said Baugh to his friends, "but I do love a run for my money, though I did n't have any more chance to-day than a rabbit. I'll take my hat off to the man that got it, however, and charge it up to my tuition account."

"You big chump, you! if you had n't bet your overcoat it would n't be so bad. What possessed you to bet it?" asked Stubb, half reprovingly.

"Oh, hell, I'll not need it. It's not going to be a very cold winter, nohow," replied Baugh, as he threw up one eye toward the warm sun. "We need exercise. Let's walk back to town. Now, this is a little unexpected, but what have I got you boys for, if you can't help a friend in trouble. There's one good thing — I've got my board paid three weeks in advance; paid it this morning out of yesterday's winnings. Lucky, ain't I?"

"Yes, you're powerful lucky. You're alive, ain't you?" said Stubb, rubbing salt into his wounds.

"Now, my dear Stubby, don't get gay with the leading lady; you may get in a bad box some day and need me."

This turn of affairs was looked upon by Stubb and Arab as quite a joke on their leader. But it was no warning to them, and they continued to play their favorite games, Stubb at poker, while Arab gave his attention to monte. Things ran along for a few weeks in this manner, Baugh never wanting for a dollar or the necessary liquids that cheer the despondent. Finally they were forced to take an inventory of their cash and similar assets. The result was suggestive that they would have to return to the chuck-line, or unearth some other resource. The condition of their finances lacked little of the red-ink line.

Baugh, who had been silent during this pow-wow, finally said, "My board will have to be provided for in a few days, but I have an idea, struck it to-day, and if she works, we'll pull through to grass like four time winners."

"What is it?" asked the other two, in a chorus.

"There's a little German on a back street here, who owns a bar-room with a hotel attached. He has a mania to run for office; in fact, there's several candidates announced already. Now, the convention don't meet until

May, which is in our favor. If my game succeeds, we will be back at work before that time. That will let us out easy."

As their finances were on a parity with Baugh's, the others were willing to undertake anything that looked likely to tide them over the winter. "Leave things to me," said Baugh. " I 'll send a friend around to sound our German, and see what office he thinks he 'd like to have."

The information sought developed the fact that it was the office of sheriff that he wanted. When the name was furnished, the leader of this scheme wrote it on a card — Seigerman, Louie Seigerman, — not trusting to memory. Baugh now reduced their finances further for a shave, while he meditated how he would launch his scheme. An hour afterwards, he walked up to the bar, and asked, " Is Mr. Seigerman in?"

" Dot ish my name, sir," said the man behind the bar.

" Could I see you privately for a few minutes?" asked Baugh, who himself could speak German, though his tongue did not indicate it.

" In von moment," said Seigerman, as he laid off his white apron and called an assistant to take his place. He then led the way to a back room, used for a storehouse. " Now, mine frendt, vat ish id?" inquired Louie, when they were alone.

"My name is Baughman," said he, as he shook Louie's hand with a hearty grip. "I work for the Continental Cattle Company, who own a range in the strip adjoining the county line below here. My people have suffered in silence from several bands of cattle thieves who have headquarters in this county. Heretofore we have never taken any interest in the local politics of this community. But this year we propose to assert ourselves, and try to elect a sheriff who will do his sworn duty, and run out of this county these rustling cattle thieves. Mr. Seigerman, it would surprise you did I give you the figures in round numbers of the cattle that my company have lost by these brand-burning rascals who infest this section.

"Now to business, as you are a business man. I have come to ask you to consent to your name being presented to the county convention, which meets in May, as a candidate for the office of sheriff of this county."

As Louie scratched his head and was meditating on his reply, Baughman continued: "Now, we know that you are a busy man, and have given this matter no previous thought, so we do not insist on an immediate reply.

But think it over, and let me impress on your mind that if you consent to make the race, you will have the support of every cattle-man in the country. Not only their influence and support, but in a selfish interest will their purses be at your command to help elect you. This request of mine is not only the mature conclusion of my people, but we have consulted others interested, and the opinion seems unanimous that you are the man to make the race for this important office."

" Mr. Baughman, vill you not haf one drink mit me?" said Seigerman, as he led the way towards the bar.

"If you will kindly excuse me, Mr. Seigerman, I never like to indulge while attending to business matters. I'll join you in a cigar, however, for acquaintance' sake."

When the cigars were lighted Baugh observed, "Why, do you keep hotel? If I had known it, I would have put up with you, but my bill is paid in advance at my hotel until Saturday. If you can give me a good room by then, I'll come up and stop with you."

" You can haf any room in mine house, Mr. Baughman," said Seigerman.

As Baugh was about to leave he once more impressed on Louie the nature of his call. " Now, Mr. Seigerman," said Baughman, using

the German language during the parting conversation, "let me have your answer at the
earliest possible moment, for we want to be-
gin an active canvass at once. This is a large
county, and to enlist our friends in your behalf
no time should be lost." With a profusion of
" Leben Sie wohls " and well wishes for each
other, the " Zweibund " parted.

Stubb and Arab were waiting on a corner
for Baugh. When he returned he withheld his
report until they had retreated to the privacy
of their own room. Once secure, he said to
both: " If you would like to know what an
active, resourceful brain is, put your ear to
my head," tapping his temple with his finger,
" and listen to mine throb and purr. Everything is working like silk. I 'm going around
to board with him Saturday. I want you to
go over with me to-morrow, Stubby, and give
him a big game about what a general uprising
there is amongst the cowmen for an efficient
man for the office of sheriff, and make it
strong. I gave him my last whirl to-day in
German. Oh, he 'll run all right ; and we want
to convey the impression that we can rally the
cattle interests to his support. Put up a good
grievance, mind you ! You can both know
that I begged strong when I took this cigar in
preference to a drink."

"It's certainly a bad state of affairs we've come to when you refuse whiskey. Don't you think so, Stubby?" said Arab, addressing the one and appealing to the other. "You never refused no drink, Baugh, you know you did n't," said Stubb reproachfully.

"Oh, you little sawed-off burnt-offering, you can't see the policy that we must use in handling this matter. This is a delicate play, that can't be managed roughshod on horseback. It has food, shelter, and drink in it for us all, but they must be kept in the background. The main play now is to convince Mr. Seigerman that he has a call to serve his country in the office of sheriff. Bear down heavy on the emergency clause. Then make him think that no other name but Louie Seigerman will satisfy the public clamor. Now, my dear Stubby, I know that you are a gifted and accomplished liar, and for that reason I insist that you work your brain and tongue in this matter. Keep your own motive in the background and bring his to the front. That's the idea. Now, can you play your part?"

"Well, as I have until to-morrow to think it over, I'll try," said Stubb.

The next afternoon Baugh and Stubb sauntered into Louie's place, and received a very cordial welcome at the hands of the proprietor. Baugh introduced Stubb as a friend of his whom he had met in town that day, and who, being also interested in cattle, he thought might be able to offer some practical suggestions. Their polite refusal to indulge in a social glass with the proprietor almost hurt his feelings.

"Let us retire to the rear room for a few moments of conversation, if you have the leisure," said Baugh.

Once secure in the back room, Stubb opened his talk. "As my friend Mr. Baughman has said, I'm local manager of the Ohio Cattle Company operating in the Strip. I'm spending considerable time in your town at present, as I'm overseeing the wintering of something like a hundred saddle horses and two hundred and fifty of our thoroughbred bulls. We worked our saddle stock so late last fall, that on my advice the superintendent sent them into the State to be corn-fed for the winter. The bulls were too valuable to be risked on the range. We had over fifty stolen last season, that cost us over three hundred dollars a head. I had a letter this morning from our superintendent, asking me to unite with what seems to be a general movement to suppress this high-handed stealing that has run riot in this county in the past. Mr. Baughman has probably acquainted you with the general sentiment in cattle circles regarding what should be done. I wish to assure you further that my people stand ready to use their best endeavors to nominate a candidate who will pledge himself to stamp out this disgraceful brand-burning and cattle-rustling. The little protection shown the live-stock interests in this western country has actually driven capital out of one of the best paying industries in the West. But it is our own fault. We take no interest in local politics. Any one is good enough for sheriff with us. But this year there seems to be an awakening. It may be a selfish interest that prompts this uprising; I think it is. But that is the surest hope in politics for us. The cattle-men's pockets have been touched, their interests have been endangered. Mr. Seigerman, I feel confident that if you will enter the race for this office, it will be a walk-away for you. Now consider the matter fully, and I might add that there is a brighter future for you politically than you possibly can see. I wish I had brought our superintendent's letter with me for you to read.

" He openly hints that if we elect a sheriff in this county this fall who makes an efficient officer, he will be strictly in line for the office of United States Marshal of western Kansas and all the Indian Territory. You see, Mr. Seigerman, in our company we have as stockholders three congressmen and one United States senator. I have seen it in the papers myself, and it is a common remark Down East, so I'm told, that the weather is chilly when an Ohio man gets left. Now with these men of our company interested in you, there would be no refusing them the appointment. Why, it would give you the naming of fifty deputies — good easy money in every one of them. You could sit back in a well-appointed government office and enjoy the comforts of life. Now, Mr. Seigerman, we will see you often, but let me suggest that your acceptance be as soon as possible, for if you positively decline to enter the race, we must look in some other quarter for an available man." Leaving these remarks for Seigerman's reflections, he walked out of the room.

As Seigerman started to follow, Baugh tapped him on the shoulder to wait, as he had something to say to him. Baugh now confirmed everything said, using the German language. He added, " Now, my friend Stubb is too modest to admit who his people really are, but the Ohio Cattle Company is practically the Standard Oil Company, but they don't want it known. It's a confidence that I'm placing in you, and request you not to repeat it. Still, you know what a syndicate they

are and the influence they carry. That very
little man who has been talking to you has
better backing than any cow-boss in the West.
He's a safe, conservative fellow to listen to."

When they had rejoined Stubb in the bar-
room, Baugh said to Seigerman, "Don't you
think you can give us your answer by Friday
next, so your name can be announced in the
papers, and an active canvass begun without
further loss of time?"

"Shentlemens, I'll dry do," said Louie,
"but you will not dake a drink mit me once
again, aind it?"

"No, thank you, Mr. Seigerman," replied
Stubb.

"He gave me a very fine cigar yesterday;
you'll like them if you try one," said Baugh
to Stubb. "Let it be a cigar to-day, Mr.
Seigerman."

As Baugh struck a match to light his cigar,
he said to Stubb, "I'm coming up to stop
with Mr. Seigerman to-morrow. Why don't
you join us?"

"I vould be wery much bleased to haf you
mine guest," said Louie, every inch the host.

"This is a very home-like looking place,"
remarked Stubb. "I may come up; I'll come
around Sunday and take dinner with you, anyhow."

"Do, blease," urged Louie.

There was a great deal to be said, and it required two languages to express it all, but finally the "Dreibund" parted. The next day Baugh moved into his new quarters, and the day following Stubb was so pleased with his Sunday dinner that he changed at once.

"I'm expecting a man from Kansas City to-morrow," said Baugh to Louie on Sunday morning, "who will know the sentiment existing in cattle circles in that city. He'll be in on the morning train."

Stubb, in the mean time, had coached Arab as to what he should say. As Baugh and he had covered the same ground, it was thought best to have Arab Ab the heeler, the man who could deliver the vote to order.

So Monday morning after the train was in, the original trio entered, and Arab was introduced. The back room was once more used as a council chamber where the "Fierbund" held an important session.

"I did n't think there was so much interest being taken," began Arab Ab, "until my attention was called to it yesterday by the president and secretary of our company in Kansas City. I want to tell you that the cattle interests in that city are aroused. Why, our secretary showed me the figures from his books;

and in the 'Tin Cup' brand alone we shipped out three hundred and twelve beeves short, out of twenty-nine hundred and ninety-six bought two years ago. My employers, Mr. Seigerman, are practical cowmen, and they know that those steers never left the range without help. Nothing but lead or Texas fever can kill a beef. We have n't had a case of fever on our range for years, nor a winter in five years that would kill an old cow. Why, our president told me if something was n't done they would have to abandon this country and go where they could get protection. His final orders were to do what I could to get an eligible man as a candidate, which, I 'm glad to hear from my friends here, we have hopes of doing. Then when the election comes off, we must drop everything and get every man to claim a residence in this county and vote him here. I 'll admit that I 'm no good as a wire-puller, but when it comes to getting out the voters, there 's where you will find me as solid as a bridge abutment.

" Why, Mr. Seigerman, when I was skinning mules for Creech & Lee, contractors on the Rock Island, one fall, they gave me my orders, which was to get every man on the works ready to ballot. I lined them up and voted them like running cattle through a branding-chute to put on a tally-mark or vent a brand. There were a hundred and seventy-five of those dagoes from the rock-cut; I handled them like dipping sheep for the scab. My friends here can tell you how I managed voting the bonds at a little town east of here. I had my orders from the same people I'm working for now, to get out the cow-puncher element in the Strip for the bonds. The bosses simply told me that what they wanted was a competing line of railroad. And as they didn't expect to pay the obligations, only author-ize them, — the next generation could attend to the paying of them, — we got out a full vote. Well, we ran in from four to five hun-dred men from the Strip, and out of over seven hundred ballots cast, only one against the bonds. We hunted the town all over to find the man that voted against us; we wanted to hang him! The only trouble I had was to make the boys think it was a straight up Democratic play, as they were nearly all ori-ginally from Texas. Now, my friends here have told me that they are urging you to ac-cept the nomination for sheriff. I can only add that in case you consent, my people stand ready to give their every energy to this com-ing campaign. As far as funds are concerned to prosecute the election of an acceptable sheriff to the cattle interests, we would simply be flooded with it. It would be impossible to use one half of what would be forced on us. One thing I can say positively, Mr. Seigerman: they would n't permit you to contribute one cent to the expense of your election. Cattle-men are big-hearted fellows — they are friends worth having, Mr. Seigerman."

Louie drew a long breath, and it seemed that a load had been lifted from his mind by these last remarks of Arab's.

"How many men are there in the Strip?" asked Arab of the others.

"On all three divisions of the last round-up there were something like two thousand," replied Baugh. "And this county adjoins the Cattle Country for sixty miles on the north," said Arab, still continuing his musing, "or one third of the Strip. Well, gentlemen," he went on, waking out of his mental reverie and striking the table with his fist, "if there 's that many men in the country below, I 'll agree to vote one half of them in this county this fall."

"Hold on a minute, are n't you a trifle high on your estimate?" asked Stubb, the conservative, protestingly.

"Not a man too high. Give them a week's lay-off, with plenty to drink at this end of the string, and every man will come in for fifty miles either way. The time we voted the bonds won't be a marker to this election."

"He's not far wrong," said Baugh to Stubb. "Give the rascals a chance for a holiday like that, and they will come from the south line of the Strip."

"That's right, Mr. Seigerman," said Arab. "They'll come from the west and south to a man, and as far east as the middle of the next county. I tell you they will be a thousand strong and a unit in voting. Watch my smoke on results!"

"Well," said Stubb, slowly and deliberately, "I think it's high time we had Mr. Seigerman's consent to make the race. This counting of our forces and the sinews of war is good enough in advance; but I must insist on an answer from Mr. Seigerman. Will you become our candidate?"

"Shentlemens, how can I refuse to be one sheriff? The cattle-mens must be protec. I accep."

The trio now arose, and with a round of oaths that would have made the captain of a pirate ship green with envy swore Seigerman had taken a step he would never regret. After the hearty congratulation on his acceptance, they reseated themselves, when Louie, in his gratitude, insisted that on pleasant occasions like this he should be permitted to offer some refreshments of a liquid nature.

"I never like to indulge at a bar," said Stubb. "The people whom I work for are very particular regarding the habits of their trusted men."

"It might be permissible on occasions like this to break certain established rules," suggested Baugh, "besides, Mr. Seigerman can bring it in here, where we will be unobserved."

"Very well, then," said Stubb, "I waive my objections for sociability's sake."

When Louie had retired for this purpose, Baugh arose to his full dignity and six foot three, and said to the other two, bowing, "Your uncle, my dears, will never allow you to come to want. Pin your faith to the old man. Why, we'll wallow in the fat of the land until the grass comes again, gentle Annie. Gentlemen, if you are gentlemen, which I doubt like hell, salute the victor!" The refreshment was brought in, and before the session adjourned, they had lowered the contents of a black bottle of private stock by several fingers.

The announcement of the candidacy of Mr. Louis Seigerman in the next week's paper (by aid of the accompanying fiver which went with the "copy") encouraged the editor, that others might follow, to write a short, favorable editorial. The article spoke of Mr. Seigerman as a leading citizen, who would fill the office with credit to himself and the community. The trio read this short editorial to Louie daily for the first week. All three were now putting their feet under the table with great regularity, and doing justice to the vintage on invitation. The back room became a private office for the central committee of four. They were able political managers. The campaign was beginning to be active, but no adverse reports were allowed to reach the candidate's ears. He actually had no opposition, so the reports came in to the central committee.

It was even necessary to send out Arab Ab to points on the railroad to get the sentiments of this and that community, which were always favorable. Funds for these trips were forced on them by the candidate. The thought of presenting a board bill to such devoted friends never entered mine host's mind. Thus several months passed.

The warm sun and green blades of grass suggested springtime. The boys had played the rôle as long as they cared to. It had served the purpose that was intended. But they must not hurt the feelings of Seigerman, or let the cause of their zeal become known to their benefactor and candidate for sheriff. One day report came in of some defection and a rival candidate in the eastern part of the county. All hands volunteered to go out. Funds were furnished, which the central committee assured their host would be refunded whenever they could get in touch with headquarters, or could see some prominent cowman.

At the end of a week Mr. Seigerman received a letter. The excuses offered at the rich man's feast were discounted by pressing orders. One had gone to Texas to receive a herd of cattle, instead of a few oxen, one had been summoned to Kansas City, one to Ohio. The letter concluded with the assurance that Mr. Seigerman need have no fear but that he would be the next sheriff.

The same night that the letter was received by mine host, this tale was retold at a cow-camp in the Strip by the trio. The hard winter was over.

At the county convention in May, Seigerman's name was presented. On each of three ballots he received one lone vote. When the news reached the boys in the Strip, they dubbed this one vote "Seigerman's Per Cent," meaning the worst of anything, and that expression became a byword on the range, from Brownsville, Texas, to the Milk River in Montana.

III

"BAD MEDICINE"

THE evening before the Cherokee Strip was thrown open for settlement, a number of old timers met in the little town of Hennessey, Oklahoma.

On the next day the Strip would pass from us and our employers, the cowmen. Some of the boys had spent from five to fifteen years on this range. But we realized that we had come to the parting of the ways.

This was not the first time that the government had taken a hand in cattle matters. Some of us in former days had moved cattle at the command of negro soldiers, with wintry winds howling an accompaniment.

The cowman was never a government favorite. If the Indian wards of the nation had a few million acres of idle land, "Let it lie idle," said the guardian. Some of these civilized tribes maintained a fine system of public schools from the rental of unoccupied lands. Nations, like men, revive the fable of the dog and the ox. But the guardian was supreme — the cowman went. This was not unexpected to most of us. Still, this country was a home to us. It mattered little if our names were on the pay-roll or not, it clothed and fed us.

We were seated around a table in the rear of a saloon talking of the morrow. The place was run by a former cowboy. It therefore became a rendezvous for the craft. Most of us had made up our minds to quit cattle for good and take claims.

"Before I take a claim," said Tom Roll, "I'll go to Minnesota and peon myself to some Swede farmer for my keep the balance of my life. Making hay and plowing fire guards the last few years have given me all the taste of farming that I want. I'm going to Montana in the spring."

"Why don't you go this winter? Is your underwear too light?" asked Ace Gee. "Now, I'm going to make a farewell play," continued Ace. "I'm going to take a claim, and before I file on it, sell my rights, go back to old Van Zandt County, Texas, this winter, rear up my feet, and tell it to them scarey. That's where all my folks live."

"Well, for a winter's stake," chimed in Joe Box, "Ace's scheme is all right. We can get five hundred dollars out of a claim for simply staking it, and we know some good ones. That sized roll ought to winter a man with modest tastes."

"You did n't know that I just came from Montana, did you, Tom?" asked Ace. "I can tell you more about that country than you want to know. I've been up the trail this year; delivered our cattle on the Yellowstone, where the outfit I worked for has a northern range. When I remember this summer's work, I sometimes think that I will burn my saddle and never turn or look a cow in the face again, nor ride anything but a plow mule and that bareback.

"The people I was working for have a range in Tom Green County, Texas, and another one in Montana. They send their young steers north to mature — good idea, too! — but they are not cowmen like the ones we know. They made their money in the East in a patent medicine — got scads of it, too. But that's no argument that they know anything about a cow. They have a board of directors — it is one of those cattle companies. Looks like they started in the cattle business to give their income a healthy outlet from the medicine branch. They operate on similar principles as those soap factory people did here in the Strip a few years ago. About the time they learn the business they go broke and retire.

"Our boss this summer was some relation to the wife of some of the medicine people Down East. As they had no use for him back there, they sent him out to the ranch, where he would be useful.

"We started north with the grass. Had thirty-three hundred head of twos and threes, with a fair string of saddle stock. They run the same brand on both ranges — the broken arrow. You never saw a cow-boss have so much trouble; a married woman was n't a circumstance to him, fretting and sweating continually. This was his first trip over the trail, but the boys were a big improvement on the boss, as we had a good outfit of men along. My idea of a good cow-boss is a man that does n't boss any; just hires a first-class outfit of men, and then there is no bossing to do.

"We had to keep well to the west getting out of Texas ; kept to the west of Buffalo Gap. From there to Tepee City is a dry, barren country. To get water for a herd the size of ours was some trouble. This new medicine man got badly worried several times. He used his draft book freely, buying water for the cattle while crossing this stretch of desert; the natives all through there considered him the softest snap they had met in years. Several times we were without water for the stock two whole days. That makes cattle hard to hold at night. They want to get up and prowl — it makes them feverish, and then 's when they are ripe for a stampede. We had several bobles crossing that strip of country; nothing bad, just jump and run a mile or so, and then mill until daylight. Then our boss would get great action on himself and ride a horse until the animal would give out — sick, he called it. After the first little run we had, it took him half the next day to count them; then he could n't believe his own figures.

"A Val Verde County lad who counted with him said they were all right — not a hoof shy. But the medicine man's opinion was the reverse. At this the Val Verde boy got on the prod slightly, and expressed himself, saying, 'Why don't you have two of the other boys count them? You can't come within a hundred of me, or yourself either, for that matter. I can pick out two men, and if they differ five head, it 'll be a surprise to me. The way the boys have brought the cattle by us, any man that can't count this herd and not have his own figures differ more than a hundred had better quit riding, get himself some sandals, and a job herding sheep. Let me give you this pointer: if you are not anxious to have last night's fun over again, you 'd better quit counting and get this herd full of grass and water before night, or you will be cattle shy as sure as hell 's hot.'

"'When I ask you for an opinion,' answered the foreman, somewhat indignant, ' such remarks will be in order. Until then you may keep your remarks to yourself.'

"'That will suit me all right, old sport,' retorted Val Verde; 'and when you want any one to help you count your fat cattle, get some of the other boys — one that 'll let you doubt his count as you have mine, and if he admires you for it, cut my wages in two.'

" After the two had been sparring with each other some little time, another of the boys ventured the advice that it would be easy to count the animals as they came out of the water; so the order went forward to let them hit the trail for the first water. We made a fine stream, watering early in the afternoon. As they grazed out from the creek we fed them through between two of the boys. The count showed no cattle short. In fact, the Val Verde boy's count was confirmed. It was then that our medicine man played his cards wrong. He still insisted that we were cattle out, thus queering himself with his men. He was gradually getting into a lone minority, though he did n't have sense enough to realize

it. He would even fight with and curse his
horses to impress us with his authority. Very
little attention was paid to him after this, and
as grass and water improved right along nothing of interest happened.

"While crossing 'No-Man's-Land' a month
later, — I was on herd myself at the time, a
bright moonlight night, — they jumped like a
cat shot with No. 8's, and quit the bed-ground
instanter. There were three of us on guard at
the time, and before the other boys could get
out of their blankets and into their saddles the
herd had gotten well under headway. Even
when the others came to our assistance, it
took us some time to quiet them down. As
this scare came during last guard, daylight
was on us before they had quit milling, and
we were three miles from the wagon. As we
drifted them back towards camp, for fear that
something might have gotten away, most of
the boys scoured the country for miles about,
but without reward. When all had returned
to camp, had breakfasted, and changed horses,
the counting act was ordered by Mr. Medicine. Our foreman naturally felt that he would
have to take a hand in this count, evidently
forgetting his last experience in that line. He
was surprised, when he asked one of the boys
to help him, by receiving a flat refusal.

"'Why won't you count with me?' he demanded.

"'Because you don't possess common cow sense enough, nor is the crude material in you to make a cow-hand. You found fault with the men the last count we had, and I don't propose to please you by giving you a chance to find fault with me. That's why I won't count with you.'

"'Don't you know, sir, that I'm in authority here?' retorted the foreman.

"'Well, if you are, no one seems to respect your authority, as you're pleased to call it, and I don't know of any reason why I should. You have plenty of men here who can count them correctly. I'll count them with any man in the outfit but yourself.'

"'Our company sent me as their representative with this herd,' replied the foreman, 'while you have the insolence to disregard my orders. I'll discharge you the first moment I can get a man to take your place.'

"'Oh, that'll be all right,' answered the lad, as the foreman rode away. He then tackled me, but I acted foolish, 'fessing up that I couldn't count a hundred. Finally he rode around to a quiet little fellow, with pox-marks on his face, who always rode on the point, kept his horses fatter than anybody, rode a

San José saddle, and was called Californy. The boss asked him to help him count the herd.

"'Now look here, boss,' said Californy, 'I'll pick one of the boys to help me, and we'll count the cattle to within a few head. Won't that satisfy you?'

"'No, sir, it won't. What's got into you boys?' questioned the foreman.

"'There's nothing the matter with the boys, but the cattle business has gone to the dogs when a valuable herd like this will be trusted to cross a country for two thousand miles in the hands of a man like yourself. You have men that will pull you through if you'll only let them,' said the point-rider, his voice mild and kind as though he were speaking to a child.

"'You're just like the rest of them!' roared the boss. 'Want to act contrary! Now let me say to you that you'll help me to count these cattle or I'll discharge, unhorse, and leave you afoot here in this country! I'll make an example of you as a warning to others.'

"'It's strange that I should be signaled out as an object of your wrath and displeasure,' said Californy. 'Besides, if I were you, I wouldn't make any examples as you were thinking of doing. When you talk of making

an example of me as a warning to others,'
said the pox-marked lad, as he reached over,
taking the reins of the foreman's horse firmly
in his hand, 'you're a simpering idiot for
entertaining the idea, and a cowardly bluffer
for mentioning it. When you talk of unhors-
ing and leaving me here afoot in a country
a thousand miles from nowhere, you don't
know what that means, but there's no danger
of your doing it. I feel easy on that point. But
I'm sorry to see you make such a fool of
yourself. Now, you may think for a moment
that I'm afraid of that ivory-handled gun you
wear, but I'm not. Men wear them on the
range, not so much to emphasize their demands with, as you might think. If it were
me, I'd throw it in the wagon; it may get you
into trouble. One thing certain, if you ever
so much as lay your hand on it, when you are
making threats as you have done to-day, I'll
build a fire in your face that you can read the
San Francisco "Examiner" by at midnight.
You'll have to revise your ideas a trifle; in
fact, change your tactics. You're off your
reservation bigger than a wolf, when you try
to run things by force. There's lots better
ways. Don't try and make talk stick for actions,
nor use any prelude to the real play you wish
to make. Unroll your little game with the real

thing. You can't throw alkaline dust in my eyes and tell me it's snowing. I'm sorry to have to tell you all this, though I have noticed that you needed it for a long time.'

" As he released his grip on the bridle reins, he continued, 'Now ride back to the wagon, throw off that gun, tell some of the boys to take a man and count these cattle, and it will be done better than if you helped.'

" 'Must I continue to listen to these insults on every hand?' hissed the medicine man, livid with rage.

" 'First remove the cause before you apply the remedy; that's in your line,' answered Californy. 'Besides, what are you going to do about it? You don't seem to be gifted with enough cow-sense to even use a modified amount of policy in your every-day affairs,' said he, as he rode away to avoid hearing his answer.

" Several of us, who were near enough to hear this dressing-down of the boss at Californy's hands, rode up to offer our congratulations, when we noticed that old Bad Medicine had gotten a stand on one of the boys called 'Pink.' After leaving him, he continued his ride towards the wagon. Pink soon joined us, a broad smile playing over his homely florid countenance.

" ' Some of you boys must have given him a heavy dose for so early in the morning,' said Pink, 'for he ordered me to have the cattle counted, and report to him at the wagon. Acted like he did n't aim to do the trick himself. Now, as I 'm foreman,' continued Pink, 'I want you two point-men to go up to the first little rise of ground, and we 'll put the cattle through between you. I want a close count, understand. You 're working under a boss now that will shove you through hell itself. So if you miss them over a hundred, I 'll speak to the management, and see if I can't have your wages raised, or have you made a foreman or something with big wages and nothing to do.'

" The point-men smiled at Pink's orders, and one asked, ' Are you ready now?'

" ' All set,' responded Pink. ' Let the fiddlers cut loose.'

" Well, we lined them up and got them strung out in shape to count, and our point-men picking out a favorite rise, we lined them through between our counters. We fed them through, and as regularly as a watch you could hear Californy call out to his pardner 'tally!' Alternately they would sing out this check on the even hundred head, slipping a knot on their tally string to keep the hundreds. It took a full half hour to put them through, and when the rear guard of crips and dogies passed this impromptu review, we all waited patiently for the verdict. Our counters rode together, and Californy, leaning over on the pommel of his saddle, said to his pardner, 'What you got?'

" 'Thirty-three six,' was the answer.

" 'Why, you can't count a little bit,' said Californy. 'I got thirty-three seven. How does the count suit you, boss?'

" 'Easy suited, gents,' said Pink. 'But I'm surprised to find such good men with a common cow herd. I must try and have you appointed by the government on this commission that's to investigate Texas fever. You're altogether too accomplished for such a common calling as claims you at present.'

" Turning to the rest of us, he said, 'Throw your cattle on the trail, you vulgar peons, while I ride back to order forward my wagon and saddle stock. By rights, I ought to have one of those centre fire cigars to smoke, to set off my authority properly on this occasion.'

" He jogged back to the wagon and satisfied the dethroned medicine man that the cattle were there to a hoof. We soon saw the saddle horses following, and an hour afterward Pink and the foreman rode by us, big as fat cattle-buyers from Kansas City, not even knowing any one, so absorbed in their conversation were they; rode on by and up the trail, looking out for grass and water.

"It was over two weeks afterward when Pink said to us, 'When we strike the Santa Fé Railway, I may advise my man to take a needed rest for a few weeks in some of the mountain resorts. I hope you all noticed how worried he looks, and, to my judgment, he seems to be losing flesh. I don't like to suggest anything, but the day before we reach the railroad, I think a day's curlew shooting in the sand hills along the Arkansas River might please his highness. In case he'll go with me, if I don't lose him, I'll never come back to this herd. It won't hurt him any to sleep out one night with the dry cattle.'

"Sure enough, the day before we crossed that road, somewhere near the Colorado state line, Pink and Bad Medicine left camp early in the morning for a curlew hunt in the sand hills. Fortunately it was a foggy morning, and within half an hour the two were out of sight of camp and herd. As Pink had outlined the plans, everything was understood. We were encamped on a nice stream, and instead of trailing along with the herd, lay over for that day. Night came and our hunters failed to return, and the next morning we trailed forward towards the Arkansas River. Just as we went into camp at noon, two horsemen loomed up in sight coming down the trail from above. Every rascal of us knew who they were, and when the two rode up, Pink grew very angry and demanded to know why we had failed to reach the river the day before.

"The horse wrangler, a fellow named Joe George, had been properly coached, and stepping forward, volunteered this excuse: 'You all did n't know it when you left camp yesterday morning that we were out the wagon team and nearly half the saddle horses. Well, we were. And what's more, less than a mile below on the creek was an abandoned Indian camp. I was n't going to be left behind with the cook to look for the missing stock, and told the *segundo* so. We divided into squads of three or four men each and went out and looked up the horses, but it was after six o'clock before we trailed them down and got the missing animals. If anybody thinks I'm going to stay behind to look for missing stock in a country full of lurking Indians — well, they simply don't know me.'

"The scheme worked all right. On reaching the railroad the next morning, Bad Medicine authorized Pink to take the herd to Ogalalla on the Platte, while he took a train for Denver. Around the camp-fire that night, Pink gave us his experience in losing Mr. Medicine. 'Oh, I lost him late enough in the day so he could n't reach any shelter for the night,' said Pink. 'At noon, when the sun was straight overhead, I sounded him as to directions and found that he did n't know straight up or east from west. After giving him the slip, I kept an eye on him among the sand hills, at the distance of a mile or so, until he gave up and unsaddled at dusk. The next morning when I overtook him, I pretended to be trailing him up, and I threw enough joy into my rapture over finding him, that he never doubted my sincerity.'

"On reaching Ogalalla, a man from Montana put in an appearance in company with poor old Medicine, and as they did business strictly with Pink, we were left out of the grave and owly council of medicine men. Well, the upshot of the whole matter was that Pink was put in charge of the herd, and a better foreman I never worked under. We reached the company's Yellowstone range early in the fall, counted over and bade our dogies good-by, and rode into headquarters. That night I talked with the regular men on the ranch, and it was there that I found out that a first-class cow-hand could get in four months' haying in the summer and the same feeding it out in the winter. But don't you forget it, she's a cow country all right. I always was such a poor hand afoot that I passed up that country, and here I am a 'boomer.'"

"Well, boom if you want," said Tom Roll, "but do you all remember what the governor of North Carolina said to the governor of South Carolina?"

"It is quite a long time between drinks," remarked Joe, rising, "but I didn't want to interrupt Ace."

As we lined up at the bar, Ace held up a glass two thirds full, and looking at it in a meditative mood, remarked: "Isn't it funny how little of this stuff it takes to make a fellow feel rich! Why, four bits' worth under his belt, and the President of the United States can't hire him."

As we strolled out into the street, Joe inquired, "Ace, where will I see you after supper?"

"You will see me, not only after supper, but all during supper, sitting right beside you."

IV

A WINTER ROUND–UP

AN hour before daybreak one Christmas morning in the Cherokee Strip, six hundred horses were under saddle awaiting the dawn. It was a clear, frosty morning that bespoke an equally clear day for the wolf *rodeo*. Every cow-camp within striking distance of the Walnut Grove, on the Salt Fork of the Cimarron, was a scene of activity, taxing to the utmost its hospitality to man and horse. There had been a hearty response to the invitation to attend the circle drive-hunt of this well-known shelter of several bands of gray wolves. The cowmen had suffered so severely in time past from this enemy of cattle that the Cherokee Strip Cattle Association had that year offered a bounty of twenty dollars for wolf scalps.

The lay of the land was extremely favorable. The Walnut Grove was a thickety covert on the north first bottom of the Cimarron, and possibly two miles wide by three long. Across the river, and extending several miles above and below this grove, was the salt plain — an alkali desert which no wild animal, ruminant or carnivorous, would attempt to cross, instinct having warned it of its danger. At the termination of the grove proper, down the river or to the eastward, was a sand dune bottom of several miles, covered by wild plum brush, terminating in a perfect horseshoe a thousand acres in extent, the entrance of which was about a mile wide. After passing the grove, this plum-brush country could be covered by men on horseback, though the chaparral undergrowth of the grove made the use of horses impracticable. The Cimarron River, which surrounds this horseshoe on all sides but the entrance, was probably two hundred yards wide at an average winter stage, deep enough to swim a horse, and cold and rolling.

Across the river, opposite this horseshoe, was a cut-bank twenty feet high in places, with only an occasional cattle trail leading down to the water. This cut-bank formed the second bottom on that side, and the alkaline plain — the first bottom — ended a mile or more up the river. It was an ideal situation for a drive-hunt, and legend, corroborated by evidences, said that the Cherokees, when they used this outlet as a hunting-ground after their enforced emigration from Georgia, had held numerous circle hunts over the same ground after buffalo, deer, and elk.

The rendezvous was to be at ten o'clock on Encampment Butte, a plateau overlooking the entire hunting-field and visible for miles. An hour before the appointed time the clans began to gather. All the camps within twenty-five miles, and which were entertaining participants of the hunt, put in a prompt appearance. Word was received early that morning that a contingent from the Eagle Chief would be there, and begged that the start be delayed till their arrival. A number of old cowmen were present, and to them was delegated the duty of appointing the officers of the day. Bill Miller, a foreman on the Coldwater Pool, an adjoining range, was appointed as first captain. There were also several captains over divisions, and an acting captain placed over every ten men, who would be held accountable for any disorder allowed along the line under his special charge.

The question of forbidding the promiscuous carrying of firearms met with decided opposition. There was an element of danger, it was true, but to deprive any of the boys of arms on what promised an exciting day's sport was contrary to their creed and occupation; besides, their judicious use would be an essential and valuable assistance. To deny one the right and permit another, would have been to divide their forces against a common enemy; so in the interests of harmony it was finally concluded to assign an acting captain over every ten men. "I'll be perfectly responsible for any of my men," said Reese, a red-headed Welsh cowman from over on Black Bear. "Let's just turn our wild selves loose, and those wolves won't stand any more show than a coon in a bear dance."

"It would be fine satisfaction to be shot by a responsible man like you or any of your outfit," replied Hollycott, superintendent of the "L X." "I hope another Christmas Day to help eat a plum pudding on the banks of the Dee, and I don't want to be carrying any of your stray lead in my carcass either. Did you hear me?"

"Yes; we're going to have egg-nog at our camp to-night. Come down."

The boys were being told off in squads of ten, when a suppressed shout of welcome arose, as a cavalcade of horsemen was sighted coming over the divide several miles distant. Before the men were allotted and their captains appointed, the last expected squad had arrived, their horses frosty and sweaty. They were all well known west end Strippers, numbering

fifty-four men and having ridden from the
Eagle Chief, thirty-five miles, starting two
hours before daybreak.

With the arrival of this detachment, Miller
gave his orders for the day. Tom Cave was
given two hundred men and sent to the upper
end of the grove, where they were to dismount,
form in a half circle skirmish-line covering the
width of the thicket, and commence the drive
down the river. Their saddle horses were to be
cut into two bunches and driven down on either
side of the grove, and to be in readiness for
the men when they emerged from the chaparral, four of the oldest men being detailed as
horse wranglers. Reese was sent with a hundred and fifty men to left flank the grove,
deploying his men as far back as the second
bottom, and close his line as the drive moved
forward. Billy Edwards was sent with twenty
picked men down the river five miles to the
old beef ford at the ripples. His instructions
were to cross and scatter his men from the
ending of the salt plain to the horseshoe, and
to concentrate them around it at the termination of the drive. He was allowed the best
ropers and a number of shotguns, to be stationed at the cattle trails leading down to the
water at the river's bend. The remainder,
about two hundred and fifty men under Lynch,

formed a long scattering line from the left entrance of the horseshoe, extending back until it met the advancing line of Reese's pickets.

With the river on one side and this cordon of foot and horsemen on the other, it seemed that nothing could possibly escape. The location of the quarry was almost assured. This chaparral had been the breeding refuge of wolves ever since the Cimarron was a cattle country. Every rider on that range for the past ten years knew it to be the rendezvous of El Lobo, while the ravages of his nightly raids were in evidence for forty miles in every direction. It was a common sight, early in the morning during the winter months, to see twenty and upward in a band, leisurely returning to their retreat, logy and insolent after a night's raid. To make doubly sure that they would be at home to callers, the promoters of this drive gathered a number of worthless lump-jawed cattle two days in advance, and driving them to the edge of the grove, shot one occasionally along its borders, thus, to be hoped, spreading the last feast of the wolves.

By half past ten, Encampment Butte was deserted with the exception of a few old cowmen, two ladies, wife and sister of a popular cowman, and the captain, who from this point

of vantage surveyed the field with a glass.
Usually a languid and indifferent man, Miller
had so set his heart on making this drive a
success that this morning he appeared alert
and aggressive as he rode forward and back
across the plateau of the Butte. The dull,
heavy reports of several shotguns caused him
to wheel his horse and cover the beef ford
with his glass, and a moment later Edwards
and his squad were seen with the naked eye to
scale the bank and strike up the river at a gallop. It was known that the ford was saddle-
skirt deep, and some few of the men were
strangers to it; but with that passed safely he
felt easier, though his blood coursed quicker.
It lacked but a few minutes to eleven, and
Cave and his detachment of beaters were due
to move on the stroke of the hour. They had
been given one hundred rounds of six-shooter
ammunition to the man and were expected to
use it. Edwards and his cavalcade were ap-
proaching the horseshoe, the cordon seemed
perfect, though scattering, when the first faint
sound of the beaters was heard, and the next
moment the barking of two hundred six-shooters was reëchoing up and down the valley of
the Salt Fork.

The drive-hunt was on; the long yell passed
from the upper end of the grove to the mouth

of the horseshoe and back, punctuated with an occasional shot by irrepressibles. The mounts of the day were the pick of over five thousand cow-horses, and corn-fed for winter use, in the pink of condition and as impatient for the coming fray as their riders.

Everything was moving like clockwork. Miller forsook the Butte and rode to the upper end of the grove; the beaters were making slow but steady progress, while the saddled loose horses would be at hand for their riders without any loss of time. Before the beaters were one third over the ground, a buck and doe came out about halfway down the grove, sighted the horsemen, and turned back for shelter. Once more the long yell went down the line. Game had been sighted. When about one half the grove had been beat, a flock of wild turkeys came out at the lower end, and taking flight, sailed over the line. Pandemonium broke out. Good resolutions of an hour's existence were converted into paving material in the excitement of the moment, as every carbine or six-shooter in or out of range rained its leaden hail at the flying covey. One fine bird was accidentally winged, and half a dozen men broke from the line to run it down, one of whom was Reese himself. The line was not dangerously broken nor did harm result, and on their return Miller was present and addressed this query to Reese: "Who is the captain of this flank line?"

"He 'll weigh twenty pounds," said Reese, ignoring the question and holding the gobbler up for inspection.

"If you were a vealy tow-headed kid, I 'd have something to say to you, but you 're old enough to be my father, and that silences me. But try and remember that this is a wolf hunt, and that there are enough wolves in that brush this minute to kill ten thousand dollars' worth of cattle this winter and spring, and some of them will be your own. That turkey might eat a few grasshoppers, but you 're cowman enough to know that a wolf just loves to kill a cow while she 's calving."

This lecture was interrupted by a long cheer coming up the line from below, and Miller galloped away to ascertain its cause. He met Lynch coming up, who reported that several wolves had been sighted, while at the lower end of the line some of the boys had been trying their guns up and down the river to see how far they would carry. What caused the recent shouting was only a few fool cowboys spurting their horses in short races. He further expressed the opinion that the line would hold, and at the close with the cordon thickened, everything would be forced into the pocket. Miller rode back down the line with him until he met a man from his own camp, and the two changing horses, he hurried back to oversee personally the mounting of the beaters when the grove had been passed.

Reese, after the captain's reproof, turned his trophy over to some of the men, and was bringing his line down and closing up with the forward movement of the drive. On Miller's return, no fault could be found, as the line was condensed to about a mile in length, while the beaters on the points were just beginning to emerge from the chaparral and anxious for their horses. Once clear of the grove, the beaters halted, maintaining their line, while from either end the horse wranglers were distributing to them their mounts. Again secure in their saddles, the long yell circled through the plum thickets and reëchoed down the line, and the drive moved forward at a quicker pace. "If you have any doubts about hell," said Cave to Miller, as the latter rode by, "just take a little *pasear* through that thicket once and you'll come out a defender of the faith."

The buck and doe came out within sight of the line once more, lower down opposite the sand dunes, and again turned back, and a half hour later all ears were strained listening to the rapid shooting from the farther bank of the river. Rebuffed in their several attempts to force the line, they had taken to the water and were swimming the river. From several sand dunes their landing on the opposite bank near the ending of the salt plain could be distinctly seen. As they came out of the river, half a dozen six-shooters were paying them a salute in lead; but the excitability of the horses made aim uncertain, and they rounded the cut-bank at the upper end and escaped.

While the deer were making their escape, a band of antelope were sighted sunning themselves amongst the sand dunes a mile below; attracted by the shooting, they were standing at attention. Now when an antelope scents danger, he has an unreasonable and unexplainable desire to reach high ground, where he can observe and be observed — at a distance. Once this conclusion has been reached, he allows nothing to stop him, not even recently built wire fences or man himself, and like the cat despises water except for drinking purposes. So when this band of antelope decided to adjourn their *siesta* from the warm, sunny slope of a sand dune, they made an effort and did break the cordon, but not without a protest.

As they came out of the sand dunes, heading straight for the line, all semblance of control was lost in the men. Nothing daunted by the yelling that greeted the antelope, once they came within range fifty men were shooting at them without bringing one to grass. With guns empty they loosened their ropes and met them. A dozen men made casts, and Juan Mesa, a Mexican from the Eagle Chief, lassoed a fine buck, while "Pard" Sevenoaks, from the J+H, fastened to the smallest one in the band. He was so disgusted with his catch that he dismounted, ear-marked the kid, and let it go. Mesa had made his cast with so large a loop that one fore leg of the antelope had gone through, and it was struggling so desperately that he was compelled to tie the rope in a hard knot to the pommel of his saddle. His horse was a wheeler on the rope, so Juan dismounted to pet his buck. While he held on to the rope assisting his horse, an Eagle Chief man slipped up and cut the rope through the knot, and the next moment a Mexican was burning the grass, calling on saints and others to come and help him turn the antelope loose. When the rope had burned its way through his gloved hands, he looked at them in astonishment, saying, "That was one bravo buck. How come thees rope untie?" But there was none to explain, and an antelope was dragging thirty-five feet of rope in a frantic endeavor to overtake his band.

The line had been closing gradually until at this juncture it had been condensed to about five miles, or a horseman to every fifty feet. Wolves had been sighted numerous times running from covert to covert, but few had shown themselves to the flank line, being contented with such shelter as the scraggy plum brush afforded. Whenever the beaters would rout or sight a wolf, the yelling would continue up and down the line for several minutes. Cave and his well-formed circle of beaters were making good time; Reese on the left flank was closing and moving forward, while the line under Lynch was as impatient as it was hilarious. Miller made the circle every half hour or so; and had only to mention it to pick any horse he wanted from the entire line for a change.

By one o'clock the drive had closed to the entrance of the pocket, and within a mile and a half of the termination. There was yet enough cover to hide the quarry, though the extreme point of this horseshoe was a sand bar with no shelter except driftwood trees. Edwards and his squad were at their post across the river, in plain view of the advancing line. Suddenly they were seen to dismount and lie down on the brink of the cut-bank. A few minutes later chaos broke out along the line, when a band of possibly twenty wolves left their cover and appeared on the sand bar. A few rifle shots rang out from the opposite bank, when they skurried back to cover.

Shooting was now becoming dangerous. In the line was a horseman every ten or twelve feet. All the captains rode up and down begging the men to cease shooting entirely. This only had a temporary effect, for shortly the last bit of cover was passed, and there within four hundred yards on the bar was a snarling, snapping band of gray wolves.

The line was halted. The unlooked-for question now arose how to make the kill safe and effective. It would be impossible to shoot from the opposite bank without endangering the line of men and horses. Finally a small number of rifles were advanced on the extreme left flank to within two hundred yards of the quarry, where they opened fire at an angle from the watchers on the opposite bank. They proved poor marksmen, overshooting, and only succeeded in wounding a few and forcing several to take to the water, so that it became necessary to recall the men to the line.

These men were now ordered to dismount and lie down, as the opposite side would take a hand when the swimming wolves came

within range of shotguns and carbines, to say
nothing of six-shooters. The current carried
the swimming ones down the river, but every
man was in readiness to give them a welcome.
The fusillade which greeted them was like a
skirmish-line in action, but the most effective
execution was with buckshot as they came
staggering and water-soaked out of the water.
Before the shooting across the river had
ceased, a yell of alarm surged through the
line, and the next moment every man was
climbing into his saddle and bringing his arms
into position for action. No earthly power
could have controlled the men, for coming at
the line less than two hundred yards distant
was the corralled band of wolves under the
leadership of a monster dog wolf, evidently a
leader of some band, and every gun within
range opened on them. By the time they had
lessened the intervening distance by one half,
the entire band deserted their leader and retreated, but unmindful of consequences he
rushed forward at the line. Every gun was
belching fire and lead at him, while tufts of
fur floating in the air told that several shots
were effective. Wounded he met the horsemen, striking right and left in splendid savage ferocity. The horses snorted and shrank
from him, and several suffered from his ugly

thrusts. An occasional effective shot was placed, but every time he forced his way through the cordon he was confronted by a second line. A successful cast of a rope finally checked his course; and as the roper wheeled his mount to drag him to death, he made his last final rush at the horse, and, springing at the flank, fastened his fangs into a stirrup fender, when a well-directed shot by the roper silenced him safely at last.

During the excitement, there were enough cool heads to maintain the line, so that none escaped. The supreme question now was to make the kill with safety, and the line was ransacked for volunteers who could shoot a rifle with some little accuracy. About a dozen were secured, who again advanced on the extreme right flank to within a hundred and fifty yards, and dismounting, flattened themselves out and opened on the skurrying wolves. It was afterward attributed to the glaring of the sun on the white sand, which made their marksmanship so shamefully poor, but results were very unsatisfactory. They were recalled, and it was decided to send in four shotguns and try the effect of buckshot from horseback. This move was disastrous, though final.

They were ordinary double-barreled shotguns, and reloading was slow in an emergency. Many of the wolves were wounded and had sought such cover as the driftwood afforded. The experiment had barely begun, when a wounded wolf sprang out from behind an old root, and fastened upon the neck of one of the horses before the rider could defend himself, and the next moment horse and rider were floundering on the ground. To a man, the line broke to the rescue, while the horses of the two lady spectators were carried into the mêlée in the excitement. The dogs of war were loosed. Hell popped. The smoke of six hundred guns arose in clouds. There were wolves swimming the river and wolves trotting around amongst the horses, wounded and bewildered. Ropes swished through the smoke, tying wounded wolves to be dragged to death or trampled under hoof. Men dismounted and clubbed them with shotguns and carbines, — anything to administer death. Horses were powder-burnt and cried with fear, or neighed exultingly. There was an old man or two who had sense enough to secure the horses of the ladies and lead them out of immediate danger. Several wolves made their escape, and squads of horsemen were burying cruel rowels in heaving flanks in an endeavor to overtake and either rope or shoot the fleeing animals.

Disordered things as well as ordered ones have an end, and when sanity returned to the mob an inventory was taken of the drive-hunt. By actual count, the lifeless carcases of twenty-six wolves graced the sand bar, with several precincts to hear from. The promoters of the hunt thanked the men for their assistance, assuring them that the bounty money would be used to perfect arrangements, so that in other years a banquet would crown future hunts. Before the hunt dispersed, Edwards and his squad returned to the brink of the cut-bank, and when hailed as to results, he replied, " Why, we only got seven, but they are all *muy docil.* We're going to peel them and will meet you at the ford."

" Who gets the turkey? " some one asked.

" The question is out of order," replied Reese. " The property is not present, because I sent him home by my cook an hour ago. If any of you have any interest in that gobbler, I'll invite you to go home with me and help to eat him, for my camp is the only one in the Strip that will have turkey and egg-nog to-night."

V

A COLLEGE VAGABOND

THE ease and apparent willingness with which some men revert to an aimless life can best be accounted for by the savage or barbarian instincts of our natures. The West has produced many types of the vagabond, — it might be excusable to say, won them from every condition of society. From the cultured East, with all the advantages which wealth and educational facilities can give to her sons, they flocked; from the South, with her pride of ancestry, they came ; even the British Isles contributed their quota. There was something in the primitive West of a generation or more ago which satisfied them. Nowhere else could it be found, and once they adapted themselves to existing conditions, they were loath to return to former associations.

About the middle of the fifties, there graduated from one of our Eastern colleges a young man of wealthy and distinguished family. His college record was good, but close application to study during the last year had told on his general health. His ambition, coupled with a laudable desire to succeed, had buoyed up his strength until the final graduation day had passed.

Alexander Wells had the advantage of a good physical constitution. During the first year at college his reputation as an athlete had been firmly established by many a hard fought contest in the college games. The last two years he had not taken an active part in them, as his studies had required his complete attention. On his return home, it was thought by parents and sisters that rest and recreation would soon restore the health of this overworked young graduate, who was now two years past his majority. Two months of rest, however, failed to produce any improvement, but the family physician would not admit that there was immediate danger, and declared the trouble simply the result of overstudy, advising travel. This advice was very satisfactory to the young man, for he had a longing to see other sections of the country.

The elder Wells some years previously had become interested in western and southern real estate, and among other investments which he had made was the purchase of an old Spanish land grant on a stream called the Salado, west of San Antonio, Texas. These land grants were made by the crown of Spain to favorite subjects. They were known by name, which they always retained when changing ownership. Some of these tracts were princely domains, and were bartered about as though worthless, often changing owners at the card-table.

So when travel was suggested to Wells, junior, he expressed a desire to visit this family possession, and possibly spend a winter in its warm climate. This decision was more easily reached from the fact that there was an abundance of game on the land, and being a devoted sportsman, his own consent was secured in advance. No other reason except that of health would ever have gained the consent of his mother to a six months' absence. But within a week after reaching the decision, the young man had left New York and was on his way to Texas. His route, both by water and rail, brought him only within eighty miles of his destination, and the rest of the distance he was obliged to travel by stage.

San Antonio at this time was a frontier village, with a mixed population, the Mexican being the most prominent inhabitant. There was much to be seen which was new and attractive to the young Easterner, and he tarried in it several days, enjoying its novel and pic-

turesque life. The arrival and departure of
the various stage lines for the accommodation
of travelers like himself was of more than
passing interest. They rattled in from Austin
and Laredo. They were sometimes late from
El Paso, six hundred miles to the westward.
Probably a brush with the Indians, or the
more to be dreaded Mexican bandits(for these
stages carried treasure — gold and silver, the
currency of the country), was the cause of the
delay. Frequently they carried guards, whose
presence was generally sufficient to command
the respect of the average robber.

Then there were the freight trains, the motive power of which was mules and oxen. It
was necessary to carry forward supplies and
bring back the crude products of the country.
The Chihuahua wagon was drawn sometimes
by twelve, sometimes by twenty mules, four
abreast in the swing, the leaders and wheelers
being single teams. For mutual protection
trains were made up of from ten to twenty
wagons. Drivers frequently meeting a chance
acquaintance going in an opposite direction
would ask, "What is your cargo?" and the
answer would be frankly given, "Specie."
Many a Chihuahua wagon carried three or
four tons of gold and silver, generally the latter. Here was a new book for this college lad,

one he had never studied, though it was more interesting to him than some he had read. There was something thrilling in all this new life. He liked it. The romance was real; it was not an imitation. People answered his few questions and asked none in return.

In this frontier village at a late hour one night young Wells overheard this conversation: "Hello, Bill," said the case-keeper in a faro game, as he turned his head halfway round to see who was the owner of the monster hand which had just reached over his shoulder and placed a stack of silver dollars on a card, marking it to win, "I've missed you the last few days. Where have you been so long?"

"Oh, I've just been out to El Paso on a little pasear guarding the stage," was the reply. Now the little pasear was a continuous night and day round-trip of twelve hundred miles. Bill had slept and eaten as he could. When mounted, he scouted every possible point of ambush for lurking Indian or bandit. Crossing open stretches of country, he climbed up on the stage and slept. Now having returned, he was anxious to get his wages into circulation. Here were characters worthy of a passing glance.

Interesting as this frontier life was to the

young man, he prepared for his final destination. He had no trouble in locating his father's property, for it was less than twenty miles from San Antonio. Securing an American who spoke Spanish, the two set out on horseback. There were several small ranchitos on the tract, where five or six Mexican families lived. Each family had a field and raised corn for bread. A flock of goats furnished them milk and meat. The same class of people in older States were called squatters, making no claim to ownership of the land. They needed little clothing, the climate being in their favor.

The men worked at times. The pecan crop which grew along the creek bottoms was beginning to have a value in the coast towns for shipment to northern markets, and this furnished them revenue for their simple needs. All kinds of game was in abundance, including waterfowl in winter, though winter here was only such in name. These simple people gave a welcome to the New Yorker which appeared sincere. They offered no apology for their presence on this land, nor was such in order, for it was the custom of the country. They merely referred to themselves as "his people," as though belonging to the land.

When they learned that he was the son of

the owner of the grant, and that he wanted to spend a few months hunting and looking about, they considered themselves honored. The best jacal in the group was tendered him and his interpreter. The food offered was something new, but the relish with which his companion partook of it assisted young Wells in overcoming his scruples, and he ate a supper of dishes he had never tasted before. The coffee he declared was delicious.

On the advice of his companion they had brought along blankets. The women of the ranchito brought other bedding, and a comfortable bed soon awaited the Americanos. The owner of the jacal in the mean time informed his guest through the interpreter that he had sent to a near-by ranchito for a man who had at least the local reputation of being quite a hunter. During the interim, while awaiting the arrival of the man, he plied his guest with many questions regarding the outside world, of which his ideas were very simple, vague, and extremely provincial. His conception of distance was what he could ride in a given number of days on a good pony. His ideas of wealth were no improvement over those of his Indian ancestors of a century previous. In architecture, the jacal in which they sat satisfied his ideals.

The footsteps of a horse interrupted their conversation. A few moments later, Tiburcio, the hunter, was introduced to the two Americans with a profusion of politeness. There was nothing above the ordinary in the old hunter, except his hair, eyes, and swarthy complexion, which indicated his Aztec ancestry. It might be in perfect order to remark here that young Wells was perfectly composed, almost indifferent to the company and surroundings. He shook hands with Tiburcio in a manner as dignified, yet agreeable, as though he was the governor of his native State or the minister of some prominent church at home. From this juncture, he at once took the lead in the conversation, and kept up a line of questions, the answers to which were very gratifying. He learned that deer were very plentiful everywhere, and that on this very tract of land were several wild turkey roosts, where it was no trouble to bag any number desired. On the prairie portion of the surrounding country could be found large droves of antelope. During drouthy periods they were known to come twenty miles to quench their thirst in the Salado, which was the main watercourse of this grant. Once Tiburcio assured his young patron that he had frequently counted a thousand antelope during a single morning. Then there was also the javeline or peccary which abounded in endless numbers, but it was necessary to hunt them with dogs, as they kept the thickets and came out in the open only at night. Many a native cur met his end hunting these animals, cut to pieces with their tusks, so that packs, trained for the purpose, were used to bay them until the hunter could arrive and dispatch them with a rifle. Even this was always done from horseback, as it was dangerous to approach the javeline, for they would, when aroused, charge anything.

All this was gratifying to young Wells, and like a congenial fellow, he produced and showed the old hunter a new gun, the very latest model in the market, explaining its good qualities through his interpreter. Tiburcio handled it as if it were a rare bit of millinery, but managed to ask its price and a few other questions. Through his companion, Wells then engaged the old hunter's services for the following day; not that he expected to hunt, but he wanted to acquaint himself with the boundaries of the land and to become familiar with the surrounding country. Naming an hour for starting in the morning, the two men shook hands and bade each other good-night, each using his own language to express the parting, though neither one knew a word the other said. The first link in a friendship not soon to be broken had been forged.

Tiburcio was on hand at the appointed hour in the morning, and being joined by the two Americans they rode off up the stream. It was October, and the pecans, they noticed, were already falling, as they passed through splendid groves of this timber, several times dismounting to fill their pockets with nuts. Tiburcio frequently called attention to fresh deer tracks near the creek bottom, and shortly afterward the first game of the day was sighted. Five or six does and grown fawns broke cover and ran a short distance, stopped, looked at the horsemen, and then capered away.

Riding to the highest ground in the vicinity, they obtained a splendid view of the stream, outlined by the foliage of the pecan groves that lined its banks as far as the eye could follow either way. Tiburcio pointed out one particular grove lying three or four miles farther up the creek. Here he said was a cabin which had been built by a white man who had left it several years ago, and which he had often used as a hunting camp in bad weather. Feeling his way cautiously, Wells asked the old hunter if he were sure that this cabin was on and belonged to the grant. Being assured on both points, he then inquired if there was anything to hinder him from occupying the hut for a few months. On the further assurance that there was no man to dispute his right, he began plying his companions with questions. The interpreter told him that it was a very common and simple thing for men to batch, enumerating the few articles he would need for this purpose.

They soon reached the cabin, which proved to be an improvement over the ordinary jacal of the country, as it had a fireplace and chimney. It was built of logs; the crevices were chinked with clay for mortar, its floor being of the same substance. The only Mexican feature it possessed was the thatched roof. While the Americans were examining it and its surroundings, Tiburcio unsaddled the horses, picketing one and hobbling the other two, kindled a fire, and prepared a lunch from some articles he had brought along. The meal, consisting of coffee, chipped venison, and a thin wafer bread made from corn and reheated over coals, was disposed of with relish. The two Americans sauntered around for some distance, and on their return to the cabin found Tiburcio enjoying his siesta under a near-by pecan tree.

Their horses refreshed and rested, they resaddled, crossing the stream, intending to return to the ranchito by evening. After leaving the bottoms of the creek, Tiburcio showed the young man a trail made by the javeline, and he was surprised to learn that an animal with so small a foot was a dangerous antagonist, on account of its gregarious nature. Proceeding they came to several open prairies, in one of which they saw a herd of antelope, numbering forty to fifty, making a beautiful sight as they took fright and ran away. Young Wells afterward learned that distance lent them charms and was the greatest factor in their beauty. As they rode from one vantage-point to another for the purpose of sight-seeing, the afternoon passed rapidly.

Later, through the interpreter he inquired of Tiburcio if his services could be secured as guide, cook, and companion for the winter, since he had fully made up his mind to occupy the cabin. Tiburcio was overjoyed at the proposition, as it was congenial to his tastes, besides carrying a compensation. Definite arrangements were now made with him, and he was requested to be on hand in the morning. On reaching the ranchito, young Wells's decision was announced to their host of the night previous, much to the latter's satisfaction. During the evening the two Americans planned to return to the village in the morning for the needed supplies. Tiburcio was on hand at the appointed time, and here unconsciously the young man fortified himself in the old hunter's confidence by intrusting him with the custody of his gun, blankets, and several other articles until he should return.

A week later found the young hunter established in the cabin with the interpreter and Tiburcio. A wagon-load of staple supplies was snugly stored away for future use, and they were at peace with the world. By purchase Wells soon had several saddle ponies, and the old hunter adding his pack of javeline dogs, they found themselves well equipped for the winter campaign.

Hunting, in which the young man was an apt scholar, was now the order of the day. Tiburcio was an artist in woodcraft as well as in his knowledge of the habits of animals and birds. On chilly or disagreeable days they would take out the pack of dogs and beat the thickets for the javeline. It was exciting sport to bring to bay a drove of these animals. To shoot from horseback lent a charm, yet made aim uncertain, nor was it advisable to get too close range. Many a young dog made a fatal mistake in getting too near this little animal, and the doctoring of crippled dogs became a daily duty. All surplus game was sent to the ranchito below, where it was always appreciated.

At first the young man wrote regularly long letters home, but as it took Tiburcio a day to go to the post-office, he justified himself in putting writing off, sometimes several weeks, because it ruined a whole day and tired out a horse to mail a letter. Hardships were enjoyed. They thought nothing of spending a whole night going from one turkey roost to another, if half a dozen fine birds were the reward. They would saddle up in the evening and ride ten miles, sleeping out all night by a fire in order to stalk a buck at daybreak, having located his range previously.

Thus the winter passed, and as the limit of the young man's vacation was near at hand, Wells wrote home pleading for more time, telling his friends how fast he was improving, and estimating that it would take at least six months more to restore him fully to his former health. This request being granted, he contented himself by riding about the country, even visiting cattle ranches south on the Frio River. Now and then he would ride into San Antonio for a day or two, but there was nothing new to be seen there, and his visits were

brief. He had acquired a sufficient knowledge of Spanish to get along now without an
interpreter.

When the summer was well spent, he began to devise some excuse to give his parents
for remaining another winter. Accordingly
he wrote his father what splendid opportuni-
ties there were to engage in cattle ranching,
going into detail very intelligently in regard
to the grasses on the tract and the fine opportunity presented for establishing a ranch.
The water privileges, the faithfulness of Tiburcio, and other minor matters were fully set
forth, and he concluded by advising that they
buy or start a brand of cattle on this grant.
His father's reply was that he should expect
his son to return as soon as the state of his
health would permit. He wished to be a duti-
ful son, yet he wished to hunt just one more
winter.

So he felt that he must make another tack
to gain his point. Following letters noted no
improvement in his health. Now, as the hunting season was near at hand, he found it convenient to bargain with a renegade doctor,
who, for the consideration offered, wrote his
parents that their son had recently consulted
him to see if it would be advisable to return
to a rigorous climate in his present condition.

Professionally he felt compelled to advise him not to think of leaving Texas for at least another year. To supplement this, the son wrote that he hoped to be able to go home in the early spring. This had the desired effect. Any remorse of conscience he may have felt over the deception resorted to was soon forgotten in following a pack of hounds or stalking deer, for hunting now became the order of the day. The antlered buck was again in his prime. His favorite range was carefully noted. Very few hunts were unrewarded by at least one or more shots at this noble animal. With an occasional visitor, the winter passed as had the previous one. Some congenial spirit would often spend a few days with them, and his departure was always sincerely regretted.

The most peculiar feature of the whole affair was the friendship of the young man for Tiburcio. The latter was the practical hunter, which actual experience only can produce. He could foretell the coming of a norther twenty-four hours in advance. Just which course deer would graze he could predict by the quarter of the wind. In woodcraft he was a trustworthy though unquoted authority. His young patron often showed him his watch and explained how it measured time, but he had no use for it. He could tell nearly enough when it was noon, and if the stars were shining he knew midnight within a few minutes. This he had learned when a shepherd. He could track a wounded deer for miles, when another could not see a trace of where the animal had passed. He could recognize the footprint of his favorite saddle pony among a thousand others. How he did these things he did not know himself. These companions were graduates of different schools, extremes of different nationalities. Yet Alexander Wells had no desire to elevate the old hunter to his own standard, preferring to sit at his feet.

But finally the appearance of blades of grass and early flowers warned them that winter was gone and that spring was at hand. Their occupation, therefore, was at an end. Now how to satisfy the folks at home and get a further extension of time was the truant's supreme object. While he always professed obedience to parental demands, yet rebellion was brewing, for he did not want to go East — not just yet. Imperative orders to return were artfully parried. Finally remittances were withheld, but he had no use for money. Coercion was bad policy to use in his case. Thus a third and a fourth winter passed, and the young hunter was enjoying life on the Salado, where questions of state and nation did not bother him.

But this existence had an end. One day in the spring a conveyance drove up to the cabin, and an elderly, well-dressed woman alighted. With the assistance of her driver she ran the gauntlet of dogs and reached the cabin door, which was open. There, sitting inside on a dry cow-skin which was spread on the clay floor, was the object of her visit, surrounded by a group of Mexican companions, playing a game called monte. The absorbing interest taken in the cards had prevented the inmates of the jacal from noticing the lady's approach until she stood opposite the door. On the appearance of a woman, the game instantly ceased. Recognition was mutual, but neither mother nor son spoke a word. Her eye took in the surroundings at a glance. Finally she spoke with a half-concealed imperiousness of tone, though her voice was quiet and kindly.

"Alexander, if you wish to see your mother, come to San Antonio, won't you, please?" and turning, she retraced her steps toward the carriage.

Her son arose from his squatting posture, hitching up one side of his trousers, then the other, for he was suspenderless, and following at a distance, scratching his head and hitching his trousers alternately, he at last managed to say, " Ah, well — why — if you can wait a few moments till I change my clothes, I 'll — I 'll go with you right now."

This being consented to, he returned to the cabin, made the necessary change, and stood before them a picture of health, bewhiskered and bronzed like a pirate. As he was halfway to the vehicle, he turned back, and taking the old black hands of Tiburcio in his own, said in good Spanish, though there was a huskiness in his voice, " That lady is my mother. I may never see you again. I don't think I will. You may have for your own everything I leave."

There were tears in the old hunter's eyes as he relinquished young Wells's hands and watched him fade from his sight. His mother, unable to live longer without him, had made the trip from New York, and now that she had him in her possession there was no escape. They took the first stage out of the village that night on their return trip for New York State.

But the mother's victory was short-lived and barren. Within three years after the son's return, he failed in two business enterprises in which his father started him. Nothing discouraged, his parents offered him a third opportunity, it containing, however, a marriage condition. But the voice of a siren, singing of flowery prairies and pecan groves on the Salado, in which could be heard the music of hounds and the clattering of horses' hoofs at full speed following, filled every niche and corner of his heart, and he balked at the marriage offer.

When the son had passed his thirtieth year, his parents became resigned and gave their consent to his return to Texas. Long before parental consent was finally obtained, it was evident to his many friends that the West had completely won him; and once the desire of his heart was secured, the languid son beamed with energy in outfitting for his return. He wrung the hands of old friends with a new grip, and with boyish enthusiasm announced his early departure.

On the morning of leaving, quite a crowd of friends and relatives gathered at the depot to see him off. But when a former college chum attempted to remonstrate with him on the social sacrifice which he was making, he turned to the group of friends, and smilingly said, " That's all right. You are honest in thinking that New York is God's country. But out there in Texas also is, for it is just as God made it. Why, I 'm going to start a cattle ranch as soon as I get there and go back to nature. Don't pity me. Rather let me pity

you, who think, act, and look as if turned out
of the same mill. Any social sacrifices which
I make in leaving here will be repaid tenfold
by the freedom and advantages of the bound-
less West."

VI

THE DOUBLE TRAIL

EARLY in the summer of '78 we were rocking along with a herd of Laurel Leaf cattle, going up the old Chisholm trail in the Indian Territory. The cattle were in charge of Ike Inks as foreman, and had been sold for delivery somewhere in the Strip.

There were thirty-one hundred head, straight "twos," and in the single ranch brand. We had been out about four months on the trail, and all felt that a few weeks at the farthest would let us out, for the day before we had crossed the Cimarron River, ninety miles south of the state line of Kansas.

The foreman was simply killing time, waiting for orders concerning the delivery of the cattle. All kinds of jokes were in order, for we all felt that we would soon be set free. One of our men had been taken sick, as we crossed Red River into the Nations, and not wanting to cross this Indian country short-handed, Inks had picked up a young fellow who evidently had never been over the trail before.

He gave the outfit his correct name, on joining us, but it proved unpronounceable, and for convenience some one rechristened him Lucy, as he had quite a feminine appearance. He was anxious to learn, and was in evidence in everything that went on.

The trail from the Cimarron to Little Turkey Creek, where we were now camped, had originally been to the east of the present one, skirting a black-jack country. After being used several years it had been abandoned, being sandy, and the new route followed up the bottoms of Big Turkey, since it was firmer soil, affording better footing to cattle. These two trails came together again at Little Turkey. At no place were they over two or three miles apart, and from where they separated to where they came together again was about seven miles.

It troubled Lucy not to know why this was thus. Why did these routes separate and come together again ? He was fruitful with inquiries as to where this trail or that road led. The boss-man had a vein of humor in his make-up, though it was not visible; so he told the young man that he did not know, as he had been over this route but once before, but he thought that Stubb, who was then on herd, could tell him how it was; he had been over the trail every year since it was laid out. This was sufficient to secure Stubb an interview, as soon as he was relieved from duty and had returned to the wagon. So Ike posted one of the men who was next on guard to tell Stubb what to expect, and to be sure to tell it to him scary.

A brief description of Stubb necessarily intrudes, though this nickname describes the man. Extremely short in stature, he was inclined to be fleshy. In fact, a rear view of Stubb looked as though some one had hollowed out a place to set his head between his ample shoulders. But a front view revealed a face like a full moon. In disposition he was very amiable. His laugh was enough to drive away the worst case of the blues. It bubbled up from some inward source and seemed perennial. His worst fault was his bar-room astronomy. If there was any one thing that he shone in, it was rustling coffin varnish during the early prohibition days along the Kansas border. His patronage was limited only by his income, coupled with what credit he enjoyed.

Once, about midnight, he tried to arouse a drug clerk who slept in the store, and as he had worked this racket before, he coppered the play to repeat. So he tapped gently on the window at the rear where the clerk slept, calling him by name. This he repeated any number of times. Finally, he threatened to have a fit; even this did not work to his advantage. Then he pretended to be very angry, but there was no response. After fifteen minutes had been fruitlessly spent, he went back to the window, tapped on it once more, saying, " Lon, lie still, you little son-of-a-sheep-thief," which may not be what he said, and walked away. A party who had forgotten his name was once inquiring for him, describing him thus, " He 's a little short, fat fellow, sits around the Maverick Hotel, talks cattle talk, and punishes a power of whiskey."

So before Stubb had even time to unsaddle his horse, he was approached to know the history of these two trails.

" Well," said Stubb somewhat hesitatingly, " I never like to refer to it. You see, I killed a man the day that right-hand trail was made: I 'll tell you about it some other time."

" But why not now? " said Lucy, his curiosity aroused, as keen as a woman's.

" Some other day," said Stubb. " But did you notice those three graves on the last ridge of sand-hills to the right as we came out of the Cimarron bottoms yesterday? You did? Their tenants were killed over that trail; you see now why I hate to refer to it, don't you? I was afraid to go back to Texas for three years afterward."

" But why not tell me? " said the young man.

" Oh," said Stubb, as he knelt down to put a hobble on his horse, " it would injure my reputation as a peaceable citizen, and I don't mind telling you that I expect to marry soon."

Having worked up the proper interest in his listener, besides exacting a promise that he would not repeat the story where it might do injury to him, he dragged his saddle up to the camp-fire. Making a comfortable seat with it, he riveted his gaze on the fire, and with a splendid sang-froid reluctantly told the history of the double trail.

" You see," began Stubb, " the Chisholm route had been used more or less for ten years. This right-hand trail was made in '73. I bossed that year from Van Zandt County, for old Andy Erath, who, by the way, was a dead square cowman with not a hide-bound idea in his make-up. Son, it was a pleasure to know old Andy. You can tell he was a good man, for if he ever got a drink too much, though he would never mention her otherwise, he always praised his wife. I 've been with him up beyond the Yellowstone, two thousand miles from home, and you always knew when the old man was primed. He would praise his wife, and would call on us boys to confirm the fact that Mary, his wife, was a good woman.

" That year we had the better of twenty-nine hundred head, all steer cattle, threes and up, a likely bunch, better than these we are shadowing now. You see, my people are not driving this year, which is the reason that I am making a common hand with Inks. If I was to lay off a season, or go to the seacoast, I might forget the way. In those days I always hired my own men. The year that this right-hand trail was made, I had an outfit of men who would rather fight than eat; in fact, I selected them on account of their special fitness in the use of firearms. Why, Inks here could n't have cooked for my outfit that season, let alone rode. There was no particular incident worth mentioning till we struck Red River, where we overtook five or six herds that were laying over on account of a freshet in the river. I would n't have a man those days who was not as good in the water as out. When I rode up to the river, one or two of my men were with me. It looked red and muddy and rolled just a trifle, but I ordered one of the boys to hit it on his horse, to see what it was like. Well, he never wet the seat of his saddle going or coming, though his horse was in swimming water good sixty yards. All the other bosses rode up, and each one examined his peg to see if the rise was falling. One fellow named Bob Brown, boss-man for John Blocker, asked me what I thought about the crossing. I said to him, 'If this ferryman can cross our wagon for me, and you fellows will open out a little and let me in, I'll show you all a crossing, and it'll be no miracle either.'

"Well, the ferryman said he'd set the wagon over, so the men went back to bring up the herd. They were delayed some little time, changing to their swimming horses. It was nearly an hour before the herd came up, the others opening out, so as to give us a clear field, in case of a mill or balk. I never had to give an order; my boys knew just what to do. Why, there's men in this outfit right now that couldn't have greased my wagon that year.

"Well, the men on the points brought the herd to the water with a good head on, and before the leaders knew it, they were halfway across the channel, swimming like fish. The swing-men fed them in, free and plenty. Most of my outfit took to the water, and kept the cattle from drifting downstream. The boys from the other herds — good men, too — kept shooting them into the water, and inside fifteen minutes' time we were in the big Injun Territory. After crossing the saddle stock and the wagon, I swam my horse back to the Texas side. I wanted to eat dinner with Blocker's man, just to see how they fed. Might want to work for him some time, you see. I pretended that I'd help him over if he wanted to cross, but he said his dogies could never breast that water. I remarked to him at dinner, 'You're feeding a mite better this year, ain't you?' 'Not that I can notice,' he replied, as the cook handed him a tin plate heaping with navy beans, 'and I'm eating rather regular with the wagon, too.' I killed time around for a while, and then we rode down to the river together. The cattle had tramped out his peg, so after setting a new one, and pow-wowing around, I told him good-by and said to him, 'Bob, old man, when I hit Dodge, I'll take a drink and think of you back here on the trail, and regret that you are not with me, so as to make it two-handed.' We said our 'so-longs' to each other, and I gave the gray his head and he took the water like a duck. He could outswim any horse I ever saw, but I drowned him in the Washita two weeks later. Yes, tangled his feet in some vines in a sunken treetop, and the poor fellow's light went out. My own candle came near being snuffed. I never felt so bad over a little thing since I burned my new red topboots when I was a kid, as in drownding that horse.

"There was nothing else worth mentioning until we struck the Cimarron back here, where we overtook a herd of Chisholm's that had come in from the east. They had crossed through the Arbuckle Mountains — came in over the old Whiskey Trail. Here was another herd waterbound, and the boss-man was as important as a hen with one chicken. He told me that the river wouldn't be fordable for a week; wanted me to fall back at least five miles; wanted all this river bottom for his cattle; said he didn't need any help to cross his herd, though he thanked me for the offer with an air of contempt. I informed him that our cattle were sold for delivery on the North Platte, and that we wanted to go through on time. I assured him if he would drop his cattle a mile down the river, it would give us plenty of room. I told him plainly that our cattle, horses, and men could all swim, and that we never let a little thing like swimming water stop us.

" No ! No ! he could n't do that ; we might as well fall back and take our turn. 'Oh, well,' said I, 'if you want to act contrary about it,

I'll go up to the King-Fisher crossing, only three miles above here. I've almost got time to cross yet this evening.'

"Then he wilted and inquired, 'Do you think I can cross if it swims them any?'

"'I'm not doing your thinking, sir,' I answered, ' but I'll bring up eight or nine good men and help you rather than make a six-mile elbow.' I said this with some spirit and gave him a mean look.

"' All right,' said he, 'bring up your boys, say eight o'clock, and we will try the ford. Let me add right here,' he continued, 'and I'm a stranger to you, young man, but my outfit don't take anybody's slack, and as I am older than you, let me give you this little bit of advice : when you bring your men here in the morning, don't let them whirl too big a loop, or drag their ropes looking for trouble, for I've got fellows with me that don't turn out of the trail for anybody.'

"' All right, sir,' I said. 'Really, I'm glad to hear that you have some good men, still I'm pained to find them on the wrong side of the river for travelers. But I'll be here in the morning,' I called back as I rode away. So telling my boys that we were likely to have some fun in the morning, and what to expect, I gave it no further attention. When we were catching up our horses next morning for the day, I ordered two of my lads on herd, which was a surprise to them, as they were both handy with a gun. I explained it to them all,— that we wished to avoid trouble, but if it came up unavoidable, to overlook no bets — to copper every play as it fell.

"We got to the river too early to suit Chisholm's boss-man. He seemed to think that his cattle would take the water better about ten o'clock. To kill time my boys rode across and back several times to see what the water was like. 'Well, any one that would let as little swimming water as that stop them must be a heap sight sorry outfit,' remarked one-eyed Jim Reed, as he rode out of the river, dismounting to set his saddle forward and tighten his cinches, not noticing that this foreman heard him. I rode around and gave him a look, and he looked up at me and muttered, 'Scuse me, boss, I plumb forgot!' Then I rode back and apologized to this boss-man: 'Don't pay any attention to my boys; they are just showing off, and are a trifle windy this morning.'

"'That's all right,' he retorted, 'but don't forget what I told you yesterday, and let it be enough said.'

"'Well, let's put the cattle in,' I urged, seeing that he was getting hot under the collar. 'We're burning daylight, pardner.'

"'Well, I'm going to cross my wagon first,' said he.

"'That's a good idea,' I answered. 'Bring her up.' Their cook seemed to have a little sense, for he brought up his wagon in good shape. We tied some guy ropes to the upper side, and taking long ropes from the end of the tongue to the pommels of our saddles, the ease with which we set that commissary over did n't trouble any one but the boss-man, whose orders were not very distinct from the distance between banks. It was a good hour then before he would bring up his cattle. The main trouble seemed to be to devise means to keep their guns and car-tridges dry, as though that was more impor-tant than getting the whole herd of nearly thirty-five hundred cattle over. We gave them a clean cloth until they needed us, but as they came up we divided out and were ready to give the lead a good push. If a cow changed his mind about taking a swim that morning, he changed it right back and took it. For in less than twenty minutes' time they were all over, much to the surprise of the boss and his men; besides, their weapons were quite dry; just the splash had wet them.

"I told the boss that we would not need any help to cross ours, but to keep well out of our way, as we would try and cross by noon, which ought to give him a good five-mile start. Well, we crossed and nooned, lying around on purpose to give them a good lead, and when we hit the trail back in these sand-hills, there he was, not a mile ahead, and you can see there was no chance to get around. I intended to take the Dodge trail, from this creek where we are now, but there we were, blocked in! I was getting a trifle wolfish over the way they were acting, so I rode forward to see what the trouble was.

"'Oh, I'm in no hurry. You're driving too fast. This is your first trip, isn't it?' he inquired, as he felt of a pair of checked pants drying on the wagon wheel.

"'Don't you let any idea like that disturb your Christian spirit, old man,' I replied with some resentment. 'But if you think I am driving too fast, you might suggest some creek where I could delude myself with the idea, for a week or so, that it was not fordable.'

"Assuming an air of superiority he observed, 'You seem to have forgot what I said to you yesterday.'

"'No, I haven't,' I answered, 'but are you going to stay all night here?'

"'I certainly am, if that's any satisfaction to you,' he answered.

"I got off my horse and asked him for a match, though I had plenty in my pocket, to light a cigarette which I had rolled during the conversation. I had no gun on, having left mine in our wagon, but fancied I'd stir him up and see how bad he really was. I thought it best to stroke him with and against the fur, try and keep on neutral ground, so I said, —

"'You ain't figuring none that in case of a run to-night we're a trifle close together for cow-herds. Besides, my men on a guard last night heard gray wolves in these sand-hills. They are liable to show up to-night. Did n't I notice some young calves among your cattle this morning? Young calves, you know, make larruping fine eating for grays.'

"'Now, look here, Shorty,' he said in a patronizing tone, as though he might let a little of his superior cow-sense shine in on my darkened intellect, 'I have n't asked you to crowd up here on me. You are perfectly at liberty to drop back to your heart's content. If wolves bother us to-night, you stay in your blankets snug and warm, and pleasant dreams of old sweethearts on the Trinity to you. We won't need you. We'll try and worry along without you.'

"Two or three of his men laughed gruffly at these remarks, and threw leer-eyed looks at me. I asked one who seemed bad, what calibre his gun was. 'Forty-five ha'r trigger,' he answered. I nosed around over their plunder purpose. They had things drying around like Bannock squaws jerking venison.

"When I got on my horse, I said to the boss, 'I want to pass your outfit in the morning, as you are in no hurry and I am.'

"'That will depend,' said he.

"'Depend on what?' I asked.

"'Depend on whether we are willing to let you,' he snarled.

"I gave him as mean a look as I could command and said tauntingly, 'Now, look here, old girl: there's no occasion for you to tear your clothes with me this way. Besides, I sometimes get on the prod myself, and when I do, I don't bar no man, Jew nor Gentile, horse, mare or gelding. You may think different, but I'm not afraid of any man in your outfit, from the gimlet to the big auger. I've tried to treat you white, but I see I've failed. Now I want to give it out to you straight and cold, that I'll pass you to-morrow, or mix two herds trying. Think it over to-night and nominate your choice — be a gentleman or a hog. Let your own sweet will determine which.'

"I rode away in a walk, to give them a chance to say anything they wanted to, but there were no further remarks. My men were all hopping mad when I told them, but I promised them that to-morrow we would fix them plenty or use up our supply of cartridges if necessary. We dropped back a mile off the trail and camped for the night. Early the next morning I sent one of my boys out on the highest sand dune to Injun around and see what they were doing. After being gone for an hour he came back and said they had thrown their cattle off the bed-ground up the trail, and were pottering around like as they aimed to move. Breakfast over, I sent him back again to make sure, for I wanted yet to avoid trouble if they did n't draw it on. It was another hour before he gave us the signal to come on. We were nicely strung out where you saw those graves on that last ridge of sand-hills, when there they were about a mile ahead of us, moseying along. This side of Chapman's, the Indian trader's store, the old route turns to the right and follows up this black-jack ridge. We kept up close, and just as soon as they turned in to the right, — the only trail there was then, — we threw off the course and came straight ahead, cross-country style, same route we came over to-day, except there was no trail there; we had to make a new one.

"Now they watched us a plenty, but it seemed they could n't make out our game. When we pulled up even with them, half a mile apart, they tumbled that my bluff of the day before was due to take effect without further notice. Then they began to circle and ride around, and one fellow went back, only hitting the high places, to their wagon and saddle horses, and they were brought up on a trot. We were by this time three quarters of a mile apart, when the boss of their outfit was noticed riding out toward us. Calling one of my men, we rode out and met him halfway. 'Young man, do you know just what you are trying to do?' he asked.

"'I think I do. You and myself as cowmen don't pace in the same class, as you will see, if you will only watch the smoke of our tepee. Watch us close, and I'll pass you between here and the next water.'

"'We will see you in hell first!' he said, as he whirled his horse and galloped back to his men. The race was on in a brisk walk. His wagon, we noticed, cut in between the herds, until it reached the lead of his cattle, when it halted suddenly, and we noticed that they were cutting off a dry cowskin that swung under the wagon. At the same time two of his men cut out a wild steer, and as he ran near their wagon one of them roped and the other heeled him. It was neatly done. I called Big Dick, my boss roper, and told him what I suspected,—that they were going to try and stampede us with a dry cowskin tied to that steer's tail they had down. As they let him up, it was clear I had called the turn, as they headed him for our herd, the flint thumping at his heels. Dick rode out in a lope, and I signaled for my crowd to come on and we would back Dick's play. As we rode out together, I said to my boys, 'The stuff's off, fellows! Shoot, and shoot to hurt!'

"It seemed their whole outfit was driving that one steer, and turning the others loose to graze. Dick never changed the course of that steer, but let him head for ours, and as they met and passed, he turned his horse and rode onto him as though he was a post driven in the ground. Whirling a loop big enough to take in a yoke of oxen, he dropped it over his off fore shoulder, took up his slack rope, and when that steer went to the end of the rope, he was thrown in the air and came down on his head with a broken neck. Dick shook the rope off the dead steer's forelegs without dismounting, and was just beginning to coil his rope when those varmints made a dash at him, shooting and yelling.

" That called for a counter play on our part, except our aim was low, for if we did n't get a man, we were sure to leave one afoot. Just for a minute the air was full of smoke. Two horses on our side went down before you could say ' Jack Robinson,' but the men were unhurt, and soon flattened themselves on the ground Indian fashion, and burnt the grass in a half-circle in front of them. When everybody had emptied his gun, each outfit broke back to its wagon to reload. Two of my men came back afoot, each claiming that he had got his man all right, all right. We were no men shy, which was lucky. Filling our guns with cartridges out of our belts, we rode out to reconnoitre and try and get the boys' saddles.

" The first swell of the ground showed us the field. There were the dead steer, and five or six horses scattered around likewise, but the grass was too high to show the men that we felt were there. As the opposition was keeping close to their wagon, we rode up to the scene of carnage. While some of the boys were getting the saddles off the dead horses, we found three men taking their last nap in the grass. I recognized them as the boss-man, the fellow with the ha'r-trigger gun, and a fool kid that had two guns on him when we were crossing their cattle the day before. One gun was n't plenty to do the fighting he was hankering for; he had about as much use for two guns as a toad has for a stinger.

"The boys got the saddles off the dead horses, and went flying back to our men afoot, and then rejoined us. The fight seemed over, or there was some hitch in the programme, for we could see them hovering near their wagon, tearing up white biled shirts out of a trunk and bandaging up arms and legs, that they had n't figured on any. Our herd had been overlooked during the scrimmage, and had scattered so that I had to send one man and the horse wrangler to round them in. We had ten men left, and it was beginning to look as though hostilities had ceased by mutual consent. You can see, son, we did n't bring it on. We turned over the dead steer, and he proved to be a stray; at least he had n't their road brand on. One-eyed Jim said the ranch brand belonged in San Saba County; he knew it well, the X — 2. Well, it was n't long until our men afoot got a remount and only two horses shy on the first round. We could stand another on the same terms in case they attacked us. We rode out on a little hill about a quarter-mile from their wagon, scattering out so as not to give them a pot shot, in case they wanted to renew the unpleasantness.

" When they saw us there, one fellow started toward us, waving his handkerchief. We began speculating which one it was, but soon made him out to be the cook; his occupation kept him out of the first round. When he came within a hundred yards, I rode out and met him. He offered me his hand and said, 'We are in a bad fix. Two of our crowd have bad flesh wounds. Do you suppose we could get any whiskey back at this Indian trader's store?'

"'If there is any man in this territory can get any I can if they have it,' I told him. 'Besides, if your lay-out has had all the satisfaction fighting they want, we'll turn to and give you a lift. It seems like you all have some dead men over back here. They will have to be planted. So if your outfit feel as though you had your belly-full of fighting for the present, consider us at your service. You're the cook, ain't you?'

"'Yes, sir,' he answered. 'Are all three dead?' he then inquired.

"'Dead as heck,' I told him.

"'Well, we are certainly in a bad box, said he meditatingly. 'But won't you all ride over to our wagon with me? I think our fellows are pacified for the present.'

"I motioned to our crowd, and we all rode over to their wagon with him. There was n't a gun in sight. The ragged edge of despair don't describe them. I made them a little talk; told them that their boss had cashed in, back over the hill; also if there was any segundo in their outfit, the position of big augur was open to him, and we were at his service.

"There was n't a man among them that had any sense left but the cook. He told me to take charge of the killed, and if I could rustle a little whiskey to do so. So I told the cook to empty out his wagon, and we would take the dead ones back, make boxes for them, and bury them at the store. Then I sent three of my men back to the store to have the boxes ready and dig the graves. Before these three rode away, I said, aside to Jim, who was one of them, 'Don't bother about any whiskey; branch water is plenty nourishing for the wounded. It would be a sin and shame to waste good liquor on plafry like them.'

"The balance of us went over to the field of carnage and stripped the saddles off their dead horses, and arranged the departed in a row, covering them with saddle blankets, pending the planting act. I sent part of my boys with our wagon to look after our own cattle for the day. It took us all the afternoon to clean up a minute's work in the morning.

"I never like to refer to it. Fact was, all the boys felt gloomy for weeks, but there was no avoiding it. Two months later, we met old man Andy, way up at Fort Laramie on the North Platte. He was tickled to death to meet us all. The herd had come through in fine condition. We never told him anything about this until the cattle were delivered, and we were celebrating the success of that drive at a near-by town.

"Big Dick told him about this incident, and the old man feeling his oats, as he leaned with his back against the bar, said to us with a noticeable degree of pride, 'Lads, I'm proud of every one of you. Men who will fight to protect my interests has my purse at their command. This year's drive has been a success. Next year we will drive twice as many. I want every rascal of you to work for me. You all know how I mount, feed, and pay my men, and as long as my name is Erath and I own a cow, you can count on a job with me.'"

"But why did you take them back to the sand-hills to bury them?" cut in Lucy.

"Oh, that was Big Dick's idea. He thought the sand would dig easier, and laziness guided every act of his life. That was five years ago, son, that this lower trail was made, and for the reasons I have just given you. No, I can't tell you any more personal experiences to-night; I 'm too sleepy."

VII

RANGERING

NO State in the Union was ever called upon to meet and deal with the criminal element as was Texas. She was border territory upon her admission to the sisterhood of States.

An area equal to four ordinary States, and a climate that permitted of outdoor life the year round, made it a desirable rendezvous for criminals. The sparsely settled condition of the country, the flow of immigration being light until the seventies, was an important factor. The fugitives from justice of the older States with a common impulse turned toward this empire of isolation. Europe contributed her quota, more particularly from the south, bringing with them the Mafia and vendetta. Once it was the Ultima Thule of the criminal western world. From the man who came for not building a church to the one who had taken human life, the catalogue of crime was fully represented.

Humorous writers tell us that it was a breach of good manners to ask a man his name, or what State he was from, or to examine the brand on his horse very particularly. It can be safely said that there was a great amount of truth mingled with the humor. Some of these fugitives from justice became good citizens, but the majority sooner or later took up former callings.

Along with this criminal immigration came the sturdy settler, the man intent on building a home and establishing a fireside. Usually following lines of longitude, he came from other Southern States. He also brought with him the fortitude of the pioneer that reclaims the wilderness and meets any emergency that confronts him. To meet and deal with this criminal element as a matter of necessity soon became an important consideration. His only team of horses was frequently stolen. His cattle ran off their range, their ear-marks altered and brands changed. Frequently it was a band of neighbors, together in a posse, who followed and brought to bay the marauders. It was an unlucky moment for a horse-thief when he was caught in possession of another man's horse. The impromptu court of emergency had no sentiment in regard to passing sentence of death. It was a question of guilt, and when that was established, Judge Lynch passed sentence.

As the State advanced, the authorities enlisted small companies of men called Rangers. The citizens' posse soon gave way to this organized service. The companies, few in number at first, were gradually increased until the State had over a dozen companies in the field. These companies numbered anywhere from ten to sixty men. It can be said with no discredit to the State that there were never half enough companies of men for the work before them.

There was a frontier on the south and west of over two thousand miles to be guarded. A fair specimen of the large things in that State was a shoe-string congressional district, over eleven hundred miles long. To the Ranger, then, is all credit due for guarding this western frontier against the Indians and making life and the possession of property a possibility. On the south was to be met the bandit, the smuggler, and every grade of criminal known to the code.

A generation had come and gone before the Ranger's work was fairly done. The emergency demanded brave men. They were ready. Not necessarily born to the soil, as a boy the guardian of the frontier was expert in the use of firearms, and in the saddle a tireless rider. As trailers many of them were equal to hounds.

In the use of that arbiter of the frontier, the six-shooter, they were artists. As a class, never before or since have their equals in the use of that arm come forward to question this statement.

The average criminal, while familiar with firearms, was as badly handicapped as woman would be against man. The Ranger had no equal. The emergency that produced him no longer existing, he will never have a successor. Any attempt to copy the original would be hopeless imitation. He was shot at at short range oftener than he received his monthly wage. He admired the criminal that would fight, and despised one that would surrender on demand. He would nurse back to life a dead-game man whom his own shot had brought to earth, and give a coward the chance to run any time if he so desired.

He was compelled to lead a life in the open and often descend to the level of the criminal. He had few elements in his make-up, and but a single purpose; but that one purpose — to rid the State of crime — he executed with a vengeance. He was poorly paid for the service rendered. Frequently there was no appropriation with which to pay him; then he lived by rewards and the friendship of ranchmen.

The Ranger always had a fresh horse at his command, — no one thought of refusing him this. Rust-proof, rugged, and tireless, he gave the State protection for life and property. The emergency had produced the man.

"Here, take my glass and throw down on that grove of timber yonder, and notice if there is any sign of animal life to be seen," said Sergeant "Smoky" C——, addressing "Ramrod," a private in Company X of the Texas Rangers. The sergeant and the four men had been out on special duty, and now we had halted after an all night's ride looking for shade and water, — the latter especially. We had two prisoners, (horse-thieves), some extra saddle stock, and three pack mules.

It was an hour after sun-up. We had just come out of the foothills, where the Brazos has its source, and before us lay the plains, dusty and arid. This grove of green timber held out a hope that within it might be found what we wanted. Eyesight is as variable as men, but Ramrod's was known to be reliable for five miles with the naked eye, and ten with the aid of a good glass. He dismounted at the sergeant's request, and focused the glass on this oasis, and after sweeping the field for a minute or so, remarked languidly, "There must be water there. I can see a band of antelope grazing out from the grove. Hold your mules! Something is raising a dust over to the south. Good! It's cattle coming to the water."

While he was covering the field with his glass, two of the boys were threatening with eternal punishment the pack mules, which showed an energetic determination to lie down and dislodge their packs by rolling.

"Cut your observations short as possible there, Ramrod, or there will be re-packing to do. Mula, you hybrid son of your father, don't you dare to lie down!"

But Ramrod's observations were cut short at sight of the cattle, and we pushed out for the grove, about seven miles distant. As we rode this short hour's ride, numerous small bands of antelope were startled, and in turn stood and gazed at us in bewilderment.

"I'm not tasty," said Sergeant Smoky, "but I would give the preference this morning to a breakfast of a well-roasted side of ribs of a nice yearling venison over the salt hoss that the Lone Star State furnishes this service. Have we no hunters with us?"

"Let me try," begged a little man we called "Cushion-foot." What his real name was none of us knew. The books, of course, would show some name, and then you were entitled to a guess. He was as quiet as a mouse, as reliable as he was quiet, and as noiseless in his movements as a snake. One of the boys went with him, making quite a detour from our course, but always remaining in sight. About two miles out from the grove, we sighted a small band of five or six antelope, who soon took fright and ran to the nearest elevation. Here they made a stand about half a mile distant. We signaled to our hunters, who soon spotted them and dismounted. We could see Cushion sneaking through the short grass like a coyote, "Conajo" leading the horses, well hidden between them. We held the antelopes' attention by riding around in a circle, flagging them. Several times Cushion lay flat, and we thought he was going to risk a long shot. Then he would crawl forward like a cat, but finally came to his knee. We saw the little puff, the band squatted, jumping to one side far enough to show one of their number down and struggling in the throes of death.

"Good long shot, little man," said the sergeant, "and you may have the choice of cuts, just so I get a rib."

We saw Conajo mount and ride up on a gallop, but we held our course for the grove. We were busy making camp when the two rode in with a fine two-year-old buck across the pommel of Cushion's saddle. They had only disemboweled him, but Conajo had the heart as a trophy of the accuracy of the shot, though Cushion had n't a word to say. It was a splendid heart shot. Conajo took it over and showed it to the two Mexican prisoners. It was an object lesson to them. One said to the other, "Es un buen tirador."

We put the prisoners to roasting the ribs, and making themselves useful in general. One man guarded them at their work, while all the others attended to the hobbling and other camp duties.

It proved to be a delightful camp. We aimed to stay until sunset, the days being sultry and hot. Our appetites were equal to the breakfast, and it was a good one.

"To do justice to an occasion like this," said Smoky as he squatted down with about four ribs in his hand, "a man by rights ought to have at least three fingers of good liquor under his belt. But then we can't have all the luxuries of life in the far West; sure to be something lacking."

"I never hear a man hanker for liquor," said Conajo, as he poured out a tin cup of coffee, "but I think of an incident my father used to tell us boys at home. He was sheriff in Kentucky before we moved to Texas. Was sheriff in the same county for twelve years. Counties are very irregular back in the old States. Some look like a Mexican brand. One of the rankest, rabid political admirers my father had lived away out on a spur of this county. He lived good thirty miles from the county seat. Did n't come to town over twice a year, but he always stopped, generally over night, at our house. My father would n't have it any other way. Talk about thieves being chummy; why, these two we have here could n't hold a candle to that man and my father. I can see them parting just as distinctly as though it was yesterday. He would always abuse my father for not coming to see him. 'Sam,' he would say, — my father's name was Sam, — 'Sam, why on earth is it that you never come to see me? I've heard of you within ten miles of my plantation, and you have never shown your face to us once. Do you think we can't entertain you? Why, Sam, I've known you since you were n't big enough to lead a hound dog. I've known you since you were n't knee to a grasshopper.'

" 'Let me have a word,' my father would put in, for he was very mild in speaking; 'let me have a word, Joe. I hope you don't think

for a moment that I would n't like to visit you ;
now do you?'

"'No, I don't think so, Sam, but you don't
come. That's why I'm complaining. You
never have come in the whole ten years you've
been sheriff, and you know that we have voted
for you to a man, in our neck of the woods.'
My father felt this last remark, though I think
he never realized its gravity before, but he
took him by one hand, and laying the other
on his shoulder said, 'Joe, if I have slighted
you in the past, I'm glad you have called my
attention to it. Now, let me tell you the first
time that my business takes me within ten
miles of your place I'll make it a point to
reach your house and stay all night, and longer
if I can.'

"'That's all I ask, Sam,' was his only reply. Now I've learned lots of the ways of the
world since then. I've seen people pleasant to
each other, and behind their backs the tune
changed. But I want to say to you fellows
that those two old boys were not throwing off
on each other — not a little bit. They meant
every word and meant it deep. It was months
afterwards, and father had been gone for a
week when he came home. He told us about
his visit to Joe Evans. It was winter time, and
mother and us boys were sitting around the

old fireplace in the evening. 'I never saw him so embarrassed before in my life,' said father. 'I did ride out of my way, but I was glad of the chance. Men like Joe Evans are getting scarce.' He nodded to us boys. 'It was nearly dark when I rode up to his gate. He recognized me and came down to the gate to meet me. "Howdy, Sam," was all he said. There was a troubled expression in his face, though he looked well enough, but he could n't simply look me in the face. Just kept his eye on the ground. He motioned for a nigger boy and said to him, "Take his horse." He started to lead the way up the path, when I stopped him. "Look here, Joe," I said to him. "Now, if there's anything wrong, anything likely to happen in the family, I can just as well drop back on the pike and stay all night with some of the neighbors. You know I'm acquainted all around here." He turned in the path, and there was the most painful look in his face I ever saw as he spoke: "Hell, no, Sam, there's nothing wrong. We've got plenty to eat, plenty of beds, no end of horse-feed, but by G——, Sam, there is n't a drop of whiskey on the place!"'

"You see it was hoss and cabello, and Joe seemed to think the hoss on him was an unpardonable offense. Salt? You'll find it in an empty one-spoon baking-powder can over there. In those panniers that belong to that big sorrel mule. Look at Mexico over there burying his fangs in the venison, will you?"

Ramrod was on guard, but he was so hungry himself that he was good enough to let the prisoners eat at the same time, although he kept them at a respectable distance. He was old in the service, and had gotten his name under a baptism of fire. He was watching a pass once for smugglers at a point called Emigrant Gap. This was long before he had come to the present company. At length the man he was waiting for came along. Ramrod went after him at close quarters, but the fellow was game and drew his gun. When the smoke cleared away, Ramrod had brought down his horse and winged his man right and left. The smuggler was not far behind on the shoot, for Ramrod's coat and hat showed he was calling for him. The captain was joshing the prisoner about his poor shooting when Ramrod brought him into camp and they were dressing his wounds. "Well," said the fellow, "I tried to hard enough, but I could n't find him. He 's built like a ramrod."

After breakfast was over we smoked and yarned. It would be two-hour guards for the day, keeping an eye on the prisoners and stock, only one man required; so we would all get plenty of sleep. Conajo had the first guard after breakfast. "I remember once," said Sergeant Smoky, as he crushed a pipe of twist with the heel of his hand, "we were camped out on the 'Sunset' railway. I was a corporal at the time. There came a message one day to our captain, to send a man up West on that line to take charge of a murderer. The result was, I was sent by the first train to this point. When I arrived I found that an Irishman had killed a Chinaman. It was on the railroad, at a bridge construction camp, that the fracas took place. There were something like a hundred employees at the camp, and they ran their own boarding-tent. They had a Chinese cook at this camp; in fact, quite a number of Chinese were employed at common labor on the road.

"Some cavalryman, it was thought, in passing up and down from Fort Stockton to points on the river, had lost his sabre, and one of this bridge gang had found it. When it was brought into camp no one would have the old corn-cutter; but this Irishman took a shine to it, having once been a soldier himself. The result was, it was presented to him. He ground it up like a machette, and took great pride in giving exhibitions with it. He was an old man

now, the storekeeper for the iron supplies, a
kind of trusty job. The old sabre renewed
his youth to a certain extent, for he used it in
self-defense shortly afterwards. This Erin-go-
bragh — his name was McKay, I think — was
in the habit now and then of stealing a pie
from the cook, and taking it into his own tent
and eating it there. The Chink kept missing his pies, and got a helper to spy out the
offender. The result was they caught the old
man red-handed in the act. The Chink armed
himself with the biggest butcher-knife he had
and went on the warpath. He found the old
fellow sitting in his storeroom contentedly
eating the pie. The old man had his eyes on
the cook, and saw the knife just in time to
jump behind some kegs of nuts and bolts.
The Chink followed him with murder in his
eye, and as the old man ran out of the tent he
picked up the old sabre. Once clear of the
tent he turned and faced him, made only one
pass, and cut his head off as though he were
beheading a chicken. They had n't yet buried
the Chinaman when I got there. I 'm willing
to testify it was an artistic job. They turned
the old man over to me, and I took him down
to the next station, where an old alcalde lived,
— Roy Bean by name. This old judge was
known as 'Law west of the Pecos,' as he

generally construed the law to suit his own
opinion of the offense. He was n't even strong
on testimony. He was a ranchman at this
time, so when I presented my prisoner he only
said, 'Killed a Chinese, did he? Well, I ain't
got time to try the case to-day. Cattle suffer-
ing for water, and three windmills out of repair. Bring him back in the morning.' I took
the old man back to the hotel, and we had a
jolly good time together that day. I never put
a string on him, only locked the door, but we
slept together. The next morning I took him
before the alcalde. Bean held court in an out-
house, the prisoner seated on a bale of flint
hides. Bean was not only judge but prose-
cutor, as well as counsel for the defense.
'Killed a Chinaman, did you?'

"'I did, yer Honor,' was the prisoner's reply.

"I suggested to the court that the prisoner
be informed of his rights, that he need not
plead guilty unless he so desired.

"'That makes no difference here,' said the
court. 'Gentlemen, I'm busy this morning.
I've got to raise the piping out of a two-hun-
dred-foot well to-day, — something the matter
with the valve at the bottom. I'll just glance
over the law a moment.'

"He rummaged over a book or two for a

few moments and then said, 'Here, I reckon this is near enough. I find in the revised statute before me, in the killing of a nigger the offending party was fined five dollars. A Chinaman ought to be half as good as a nigger. Stand up and receive your sentence. What's your name?'

"'Jerry McKay, your Honor.'

"Just then the court noticed one of the vaqueros belonging to the ranch standing in the door, hat in hand, and he called to him in Spanish, 'Have my horse ready, I'll be through here just in a minute.'

"'McKay,' said the court as he gave him a withering look, 'I'll fine you two dollars and a half and costs. Officer, take charge of the prisoner until it's paid!' It took about ten dollars to cover everything, which I paid, McKay returning it when he reached his camp. Whoever named that alcalde 'Law west of the Pecos' knew his man."

"I'll bet a twist of dog," said Ramrod, "that prisoner with the black whiskers sabes English. Did you notice him paying strict attention to Smoky's little talk? He reminds me of a fellow that crouched behind his horse at the fight we had on the head of the Arroyo Colorado and plugged me in the shoulder. What, you never heard of it? That's so,

Cushion has n't been with us but a few months.
Well, it was in '82, down on the river, about
fifty miles northwest of Brownsville. Word
came in one day that a big band of horse-
thieves were sweeping the country of every
horse they could gather. There was a number
of the old Cortina's gang known to be still on
the rustle. When this report came, it found
eleven men in camp. We lost little time saddling up, only taking five days' rations with us,
for they were certain to recross the river before that time in case we failed to intercept
them. Every Mexican in the country was
terrorized. All they could tell us was that
there was plenty of ladrones and lots of horses,
'muchos' being the qualifying word as to the
number of either.

"It was night before we came to their trail,
and to our surprise they were heading inland, to
the north. They must have had a contract to
supply the Mexican army with cavalry horses.
They were simply sweeping the country, taking nothing but gentle stock. These they
bucked in strings, and led. That made easy
trailing, as each string left a distinct trail. The
moon was splendid that night, and we trailed
as easily as though it had been day. We did n't
halt all night long on either trail, pegging
along at a steady gait, that would carry us

inland some distance before morning. Our scouts aroused every ranch within miles that we passed on the way, only to have reports exaggerated as usual. One thing we did learn that night, and that was that the robbers were led by a white man. He was described in the superlatives that the Spanish language possesses abundantly; everything from the horse he rode to the solid braid on his sombrero was described in the same strain. But that kind of prize was the kind we were looking for.

"On the head of the Arroyo Colorado there is a broken country interspersed with glades and large openings. We felt very sure that the robbers would make camp somewhere in that country. When day broke the freshness of the trail surprised and pleased us. They could n't be far away. Before an hour passed, we noticed a smoke cloud hanging low in the morning air about a mile ahead. We dismounted and securely tied our horses and pack stock. Every man took all the cartridges he could use, and was itching for the chance to use them. We left the trail, and to conceal ourselves took to the brush or dry arroyos as a protection against alarming the quarry. They were a quarter of a mile off when we first sighted them. We began to think the reports were right, for there seemed no end of horses, and at least twenty-five men. By dropping back we could gain one of those dry arroyos which would bring us within one hundred yards of their camp. A young fellow by the name of Rusou, a crack shot, was acting captain in the absence of our officers. As we backed into the arroyo he said to us, 'If there's a white man there, leave him to me.' We were all satisfied that he would be cared for properly at Rusou's hands, and silence gave consent.

"Opposite the camp we wormed out of the arroyo like a skirmish line, hugging the ground for the one remaining little knoll between the robbers and ourselves. I was within a few feet of Rusou as we sighted the camp about seventy-five yards distant. We were trying to make out a man that was asleep, at least he had his hat over his face, lying on a blanket with his head in a saddle. We concluded he was a white man, if there was one. Our survey of their camp was cut short by two shots fired at us by two pickets of theirs posted to our left about one hundred yards. No one was hit, but the sleeping man jumped to his feet with a six-shooter in each hand. I heard Rusou say to himself, 'You're too late, my friend.' His carbine spoke, and the fellow fell forward, firing both guns into the ground at his feet as he went down.

" Then the stuff was off and she opened up in earnest. They fought all right. I was on my knee pumping lead for dear life, and as I threw my carbine down to refill the magazine, a bullet struck it in the heel of the magazine with sufficient force to knock me backward. I thought I was hit for an instant, but it passed away in a moment. When I tried to work the lever I saw that my carbine was ruined. I called to the boys to notice a fellow with black whiskers who was shooting from behind his horse. He would shoot over and under alternately. I thought he was shooting at me. I threw down my carbine and drew my six-shooter. Just then I got a plug in the shoulder, and things got dizzy and dark. It caught me an inch above the nipple, ranging upward, — shooting from under, you see. But some of the boys must have noticed him, for he decorated the scene badly leaded, when it was over. I was unconscious for a few minutes, and when I came around the fight had ended.

" During the few brief moments that I was knocked out, our boys had closed in on them and mixed it with them at short range. The thieves took to such horses as they could lay their hands on, and one fellow went no farther. A six-shooter halted him at fifty yards. The boys rounded up over a hundred horses, each one with a fiber grass halter on, besides killing over twenty wounded ones to put them out of their misery.

"It was a nasty fight. Two of our own boys were killed and three were wounded. But then you ought to have seen the other fellows; we took no prisoners that day. Nine men lay dead. Horses were dead and dying all around, and the wounded ones were crying in agony.

"This white man proved to be a typical dandy, a queer leader for such a gang. He was dressed in buckskin throughout, while his sombrero was as fine as money could buy. You can know it was a fine one, for it was sold for company prize money, and brought three hundred and fifty dollars. He had nearly four thousand dollars on his person and in his saddle. A belt which we found on him had eleven hundred in bills and six hundred in good old yellow gold. The silver in the saddle was mixed, Mexican and American about equally.

"He had as fine a gold watch in his pocket as you ever saw, while his firearms and saddle were beauties. He was a dandy all right, and a fine-looking man, over six feet tall, with swarthy complexion and hair like a raven's wing. He was too nice a man for the company he was in. We looked the 'Black Book' over afterward for any description of him. At that time there were over four thousand criminals and outlaws described in it, but there was no description that would fit him. For this reason we supposed that he must live far in the interior of Mexico.

"Our saddle stock was brought up, and our wounded were bandaged as best they could be. My wound was the worst, so they concluded to send me back. One of the boys went with me, and we made a fifty-mile ride before we got medical attention. While I was in the hospital I got my divvy of the prize money, something over four hundred dollars."

When Ramrod had finished his narrative, he was compelled to submit to a cross-examination at the hands of Cushion-foot, for he delighted in a skirmish. All his questions being satisfactorily answered, Cushion-foot drew up his saddle alongside of where Ramrod lay stretched on a blanket, and seated himself. This was a signal to the rest of us that he had a story, so we drew near, for he spoke so low that you must be near to hear him. His years on the frontier were rich in experience, though he seldom referred to them.

Addressing himself to Ramrod, he began: "You might live amongst these border Mexicans all your life and think you knew them; but every day you live you'll see new fea-

tures about them. You can't calculate on them
with any certainty. What they ought to do
by any system of reasoning they never do.
They will steal an article and then give it
away. You 've heard the expression 'robbing
Peter to pay Paul.' Well, my brother played
the rôle of Paul once himself. It was out in
Arizona at a place called Las Palomas. He
was a stripling of a boy, but could palaver
Spanish in a manner that would make a Mexican ashamed of his ancestry. He was about
eighteen at this time and was working in a
store. One morning as he stepped outside the
store, where he slept, he noticed quite a com-
motion over around the custom-house. He
noticed that the town was full of strangers, as
he crossed over toward the crowd. He was
suddenly halted and searched by a group of
strange men. Fortunately he had no arms on
him, and his ability to talk to them, together
with his boyish looks, ingratiated him in their
favor, and they simply made him their prisoner.
Just at that moment an alcalde rode up to the
group about him, and was ordered to halt.
He saw at a glance they were revolutionists,
and whirling his mount attempted to escape,
when one of them shot him from his horse.
The young fellow then saw what he was into.

"They called themselves Timochis. They

belonged in Mexico, and a year or so before
they refused to pay taxes that the Mexican
government levied on them, and rebelled.
Their own government sent soldiers after
them, resulting in about eight hundred soldiers being killed, when they dispersed into
small bands, one of which was paying Las
Palomas a social call that morning. Along
the Rio Grande it is only a short step at best
from revolution to robbery, and either calling
has its variations.

"Well, they took my brother with them to
act as spokesman in looting the town. The
custom-house was a desired prize, and when
my brother interpreted their desires to the
collector, he consented to open the safe, as life
had charms for him, even in Arizona. Uncle
Sam's strong-box yielded up over a thousand
dobes. They turned their attention to the few
small stores of the town, looting them of the
money and goods as they went. There was
quite a large store kept by a Frenchman, who
refused to open, when he realized that the
Timochi was honoring the town with his presence. They put the boy in the front and ordered him to call on the Frenchman to open
up. He said afterward that he put in a word
for himself, telling him not to do any shooting through the door. After some persuasion

the store was opened and proved to be quite a prize. Then they turned their attention to the store where the boy worked. He unlocked it and waved them in. He went into the cellar and brought up half a dozen bottles of imported French Cognac, and invited the chief bandit and his followers to be good enough to join him. In the mean time they had piled up on the counters such things as they wanted. They made no money demand on him, the chief asking him to set a price on the things they were taking. He made a hasty inventory of the goods and gave the chief the figures, about one hundred and ten dollars. The chief opened a sack that they had taken from the custom-house and paid the bill with a flourish.

"The chief then said that he had a favor to ask: that my brother should cheer for the revolutionists, to identify him as a friend. That was easy, so he mounted the counter and gave three cheers of 'Viva los Timochis!' He got down off the counter, took the bandit by the arm, and led him to the rear, where with glasses in the air they drank to 'Viva los Timochis!' again. Then the chief and his men withdrew and recrossed the river. It was the best day's trade he had had in a long time. Now, here comes in the native. While the boy did everything from compulsion and policy, the native element looked upon him with suspicion. The owners of the store, knowing that this suspicion existed, advised him to leave, and he did."

The two prisoners were sleeping soundly. Sleep comes easily to tired men, and soon all but the solitary guard were wrapped in sleep, to fight anew in rangers' dreams scathless battles!

There was not lacking the pathetic shade in the redemption of this State from crime and lawlessness. In the village burying-ground of Round Rock, Texas, is a simple headstone devoid of any lettering save the name "Sam Bass." His long career of crime and lawlessness would fill a good-sized volume. He met his death at the hands of Texas Rangers. Years afterward a woman, with all the delicacy of her sex, and knowing the odium that was attached to his career, came to this town from her home in the North and sought out his grave. As only a woman can, when some strong tie of affection binds, this woman went to work to mark the last resting-place of the wayward man. Concealing her own identity, she performed these sacred rites, clothing in mystery her relation to the criminal. The people of the village would not have withheld their services in well-meant friendship, but she shrank from them, being a stranger.

A year passed, and she came again. This time she brought the stone which marks his last resting-place. The chivalry of this generous people was aroused in admiration of a woman that would defy the calumny attached to an outlaw. While she would have shrunk from kindness, had she been permitted, such devotion could not go unchallenged. So she disclosed her identity.

She was his sister.

Bass was Northern born, and this sister was the wife of a respectable practicing physician in Indiana. Womanlike, her love for a wayward brother followed him beyond his disgraceful end. With her own hands she performed an act that has few equals, as a testimony of love and affection for her own.

For many years afterward she came annually, her timidity having worn away after the generous reception accorded her at the hands of a hospitable people.

VIII

AT COMANCHE FORD

THERE'S our ford," said Juan, — our half-blood trailer, — pointing to the slightest sag in a low range of hills distant twenty miles.

We were Texas Rangers. It was nearly noon of a spring day, and we had halted on sighting our destination, — Comanche Ford on the Concho River. Less than three days before, we had been lounging around camp, near Tepee City, one hundred and seventy-five miles northeast of our present destination. A courier had reached us with an emergency order, which put every man in the saddle within an hour after its receipt.

An outfit with eight hundred cattle had started west up the Concho. Their destination was believed to be New Mexico. Suspicion rested on them, as they had failed to take out inspection papers for moving the cattle, and what few people had seen them declared that one half the cattle were brand burnt or blotched beyond recognition. Besides, they had an outfit of twenty heavily armed men, or twice as many as were required to manage a herd of that size.

Our instructions were to make this crossing with all possible haste, and if our numbers were too few, there to await assistance before dropping down the river to meet the herd. When these courier orders reached us at Tepee, they found only twelve men in camp, with not an officer above a corporal. Fortunately we had Dad Root with us, a man whom every man in our company would follow as though he had been our captain. He had not the advantage in years that his name would indicate, but he was an exceedingly useful man in the service. He could resight a gun, shoe a horse, or empty a six-shooter into a tree from the back of a running horse with admirable accuracy. In dressing a gun-shot wound, he had the delicate touch of a woman. Every man in the company went to him with his petty troubles, and came away delighted. Therefore there was no question as to who should be our leader on this raid; no one but Dad was even considered.

Sending a brief note to the adjutant-general by this same courier, stating that we had started with twelve men, we broke camp, and in less than an hour were riding southwest. One thing which played into our hands in making this forced ride was the fact that we had a number of extra horses on hand. For a few months previous we had captured quite a number of stolen horses, and having no chance to send into the settlements where they belonged, we used them as extra riding horses. With our pack mules light and these extra saddlers for a change, we covered the country rapidly. Sixteen hours a day in the saddle makes camp-fires far apart. Dad, too, could always imagine that a few miles farther on we would find a fine camping spot, and his views were law to us.

We had been riding hard for an hour across a tableland known as Cibollo Mesa, and now for the first time had halted at sighting our destination, yet distant three hours' hard riding. "Boys," said Dad, "we'll make it early to-day. I know a fine camping spot near a big pool in the river. After supper we'll all take a swim, and feel as fresh as pond-lilies."

"Oh, we swim this evening, do we?" inquired Orchard. "That's a Christian idea, Dad, cleanliness, you know. Do we look as though a swim would improve our good looks?" The fact that, after a ride like the one we were near finishing, every man of us was saturated with fine alkaline dust, made the latter question ludicrous.

For this final ride we changed horses for the last time on the trip, and after a three hours' ride under a mid-day torrid sun, the shade of Concho's timber and the companionship of running water were ours. We rode with a whoop into the camp which Dad had had in his mind all morning, and found it a paradise. We fell out of our saddles, and tired horses were rolling and groaning all around us in a few minutes. The packs were unlashed with the same alacrity, while horses, mules, and men hurried to the water. With the exception of two horses on picket, it was a loose camp in a few moments' time. There was no thought of eating now, with such inviting swimming pools as the spring freshets had made.

Dad soon located the big pool, for he had been there before, and shortly a dozen men floundered and thrashed around in it like a school of dolphins. On one side of the pool was a large sloping rock, from which splendid diving could be had. On this rock we gathered like kid goats on a stump, or sunned ourselves like lizards. To get the benefit of the deepest water, only one could dive at a time. We were so bronzed from the sun that when undressed the protected parts afforded a striking contrast to the brown bands about our necks.

Orchard was sitting on the rock waiting for his turn to dive, when Long John, patting his naked shoulder, said admiringly, —

"Orchard, if I had as purty a plump shoulder as you have, I'd have my picture taken kind of half careless like — like the girls do sometimes. Wear one of those far-away looks, roll up your eyes, and throw up your head like you was listening for it to thunder. Then while in that attitude, act as if you did n't notice and let all your clothing fall entirely off your shoulder. If you'll have your picture taken that way and give me one, I'll promise you to set a heap of store by it, old man."

Orchard looked over the edge of the rock at his reflection in the water, and ventured, "Would n't I need a shave? and ought n't I to have a string of beads around my swan-like neck, with a few spangles on it to glitter and sparkle? I'd have to hold my right hand over this old gun scar in my left shoulder, so as not to mar the beauty of the picture. Remind me of it, John, and I'll have some taken, and you shall have one."

A few minutes later Happy Jack took his place on the rim of the rock to make a dive, his magnificent physique of six feet and two hundred pounds looming up like a Numidian cavalryman, when Dad observed, " How comes it, Jack, that you are so pitted in the face and neck with pox-marks, and there 's none on your body?"

"Just because they come that way, I reckon," was the answer vouchsafed. "You may think I 'm funning, lads, but I never felt so supremely happy in all my life as when I got well of the smallpox. I had one hundred and ninety dollars in my pocket when I took down with them, and only had eight left when I got up and was able to go to work." Here, as he poised on tiptoe, with his hands gracefully arched over his head for a dive, he was arrested in the movement by a comment of one of the boys, to the effect that he "could n't see anything in that to make a man so *supremely happy.*"

He turned his head halfway round at the speaker, and never losing his poise, remarked, "Well, but you must recollect that there was five of us taken down at the same time, and the other four died," and he made a graceful spring, boring a hole in the water, which seethed around him, arising a moment later throwing water like a porpoise, as though he would n't exchange his position in life, humble as it was, with any one of a thousand dead heroes.

After an hour in the water and a critical

examination of all the old gun-shot wounds of our whole squad, and the consequent verdict that it was simply impossible to kill a man, we returned to camp and began getting supper. There was no stomach so sensitive amongst us that it could n't assimilate bacon, beans, and black coffee.

When we had done justice to the supper, the twilight hours of the evening were spent in making camp snug for the night. Every horse or mule was either picketed or hobbled. Every man washed his saddle blankets, as the long continuous ride had made them rancid with sweat. The night air was so dry and warm that they would even dry at night. There was the usual target practice and the never-ending cleaning of firearms. As night settled over the camp, everything was in order. The blankets were spread, and smoking and yarning occupied the time until sleep claimed us.

"Talking about the tight places," said Orchard, "in which a man often finds himself in this service, reminds me of a funny experience which I once had, out on the head-waters of the Brazos. I 've smelt powder at short range, and I 'm willing to admit there 's nothing fascinating in it. But this time I got buffaloed by a bear.

"There are a great many brakes on the head

of the Brazos, and in them grow cedar thickets. I forget now what the duty was that we were there on, but there were about twenty of us in the detachment at the time. One morning, shortly after daybreak, another lad and myself walked out to unhobble some extra horses which we had with us. The horses had strayed nearly a mile from camp, and when we found them they were cutting up as if they had been eating loco weed for a month. When we came up to them, we saw that they were scared. These horses could n't talk, but they told us that just over the hill was something they were afraid of.

"We crept up the little hill, and there over in a draw was the cause of their fear, — a big old lank Cinnamon. He was feeding along, heading for a thicket of about ten acres. The lad who was with me stayed and watched him, while I hurried back, unhobbled the horses, and rushed them into camp. I hustled out every man, and they cinched their hulls on those horses rapidly. By the time we had reached the lad who had stayed to watch him, the bear had entered the thicket, but unalarmed. Some fool suggested the idea that we could drive him out in the open and rope him. The lay of the land would suggest such an idea, for beyond this motte of cedar lay an impenetrable thicket of over a hundred acres, which we thought he would head for if alarmed. There was a ridge of a divide between these cedar brakes, and if the bear should attempt to cross over, he would make a fine mark for a rope.

" Well, I always was handy with a rope, and the boys knew it, so I and three others who could twirl a rope were sent around on this divide, to rope him in case he came out. The others left their horses and made a half-circle drive through the grove, beating the brush and burning powder as though it did n't cost anything. We ropers up on the divide scattered out, hiding ourselves as much as we could in the broken places. We wanted to get him out in the clear in case he played nice. He must have been a sullen old fellow, for we were beginning to think they had missed him or he had holed, when he suddenly lumbered out directly opposite me and ambled away towards the big thicket.

" I was riding a cream-colored horse, and he was as good a one as ever was built on four pegs, except that he was nervous. He had never seen a bear, and when I gave him the rowel, he went after that bear like a cat after a mouse. The first sniff he caught of the bear, he whirled quicker than lightning, but I had made my cast, and the loop settled over Mr. Bear's shoulders, with one of his fore feet through it. I had tied the rope in a hard knot to the pommel, and the way my horse checked that bear was a caution. It must have made bruin mad. My horse snorted and spun round like a top, and in less time than it takes to tell it, there was a bear, a cream-colored horse, and a man sandwiched into a pile on the ground, and securely tied with a three-eighths-inch rope. The horse had lashed me into the saddle by winding the rope, and at the same time windlassed the bear in on top of us. The horse cried with fear as though he was being burnt to death, while the bear grinned and blew his breath in my face. The running noose in the rope had cut his wind so badly, he could hardly offer much resistance. It was a good thing he had his wind cut, or he would have made me sorry I enlisted. I did n't know it at the time, but my six-shooter had fallen out of the holster, while the horse was lying on my carbine.

"The other three rode up and looked at me, and they all needed killing. Horse, bear, and man were so badly mixed up, they dared not shoot. One laughed till he cried, another one was so near limp he looked like a ghost, while one finally found his senses and, dismounting, cut the rope in half a dozen places and untied the bundle. My horse floundered to his feet and ran off, but before the bear could free the noose, the boys got enough lead into him at close quarters to hold him down. The entire detachment came out of the thicket, and their hilarity knew no bounds. I was the only man in the crowd who did n't enjoy the bear chase. Right then I made a resolve that hereafter, when volunteers are called for to rope a bear, my accomplishments in that line will remain unmentioned by me. I 'll eat my breakfast first, anyhow, and think it over carefully."

"Dogs and horses are very much alike about a bear," said one of the boys. "Take a dog that never saw a bear in his life, and let him get a sniff of one, and he 'll get up his bristles like a javeline and tuck his tail and look about for good backing or a clear field to run."

Long John showed symptoms that he had some yarn to relate, so we naturally remained silent to give him a chance, in case the spirit moved in him. Throwing a brand into the fire after lighting his cigarette, he stretched himself on the ground, and the expected happened.

"A few years ago, while rangering down the country," said he, "four of us had trailed some horse-thieves down on the Rio Grande, when they gave us the slip by crossing over into Mexico. We knew the thieves were just across the river, so we hung around a few days, in the hope of catching them, for if they should recross into Texas they were our meat. Our plans were completely upset the next morning, by the arrival of twenty United States cavalrymen on the cold trail of four deserters. The fact that these deserters were five days ahead and had crossed into Mexico promptly on reaching the river, did not prevent this squad of soldiers from notifying both villages on each side of the river as to their fruitless errand. They could n't follow their own any farther, and they managed to scare our quarry into hiding in the interior. We waited until the soldiers returned to the post, when we concluded we would take a little *pasear* over into Mexico on our own account.

"We called ourselves horse-buyers. The government was paying like thirty dollars for deserters, and in case we run across them, we figured it would pay expenses to bring them out. These deserters were distinguishable wherever they went by the size of their horses; besides, they had two fine big American mules for packs. They were marked right for that country. Everything about them was *muy grande.* We were five days overtaking them, and then at a town one hundred and forty miles in the interior. They had celebrated their desertion the day previous to our arrival by getting drunk, and when the horse-buyers arrived they were in jail. This last condition rather frustrated our plans for their capture, as we expected to kidnap them out. But now we had red tape authorities to deal with.

"We found the horses, mules, and accoutrements in a corral. They would be no trouble to get, as the bill for their keep was the only concern of the corral-keeper. Two of the boys who were in the party could palaver Spanish, so they concluded to visit the alcalde of the town, inquiring after horses in general and incidentally finding out when our deserters would be released. The alcalde received the boys with great politeness, for Americans were rare visitors in his town, and after giving them all the information available regarding horses, the subject innocently changed to the American prisoners in jail. The alcalde informed them that he was satisfied they were deserters, and not knowing just what to do with them he had sent a courier that very morning to the governor for instructions in the matter. He estimated it would require at least ten days to receive the governor's reply. In the mean time, much as he regretted it, they would remain prisoners. Before parting, those two innocents permitted their host to open a bottle of wine as an evidence of the friendly feeling, and at the final leave-taking, they wasted enough politeness on each other to win a woman.

" When the boys returned to us other two, we were at our wits' end. We were getting disappointed too often. The result was that we made up our minds that rather than throw up, we would take those deserters out of jail and run the risk of getting away with them. We had everything in readiness an hour before nightfall. We explained, to the satisfaction of the Mexican hostler who had the stock in charge, that the owners of these animals were liable to be detained in jail possibly a month, and to avoid the expense of their keeping, we would settle the bill for our friends and take the stock with us. When the time came every horse was saddled and the mules packed and in readiness. We had even moved our own stock into the same corral, which was only a short distance from the jail.

" As night set in we approached the *carsel*. The turnkey answered our questions very politely through a grated iron door, and to our request to speak with the prisoners, he regretted that they were being fed at that moment, and we would have to wait a few minutes. He unbolted the door, however, and offered to show us into a side room, an invitation we declined. Instead, we relieved him of his keys and made known our errand. When he discovered that we were armed and he was our prisoner, he was speechless with terror. It was short work to find the men we wanted and march them out, locking the gates behind us and taking jailer and keys with us. Once in the saddle, we bade the poor turnkey good-by and returned him his keys.

"We rode fast, but in less than a quarter of an hour there was a clanging of bells which convinced us that the alarm had been given. Our prisoners took kindly to the rescue and rode willingly, but we were careful to conceal our identity or motive. We felt certain there would be pursuit, if for no other purpose, to justify official authority. We felt easy, for we were well mounted, and if it came to a pinch, we would burn powder with them, one round at least.

"Before half an hour had passed, we were aware that we were pursued. We threw off the road at right angles and rode for an hour.

Then, with the North Star for a guide, we put over fifty miles behind us before sunrise. It was impossible to secrete ourselves the next day, for we were compelled to have water for ourselves and stock. To conceal the fact that our friends were prisoners, we returned them their arms after throwing away their ammunition. We had to enter several ranches during the day to secure food and water, but made no particular effort to travel.

"About four o'clock we set out, and to our surprise, too, a number of horsemen followed us until nearly dark. Passing through a slight shelter, in which we were out of sight some little time, two of us dropped back and awaited our pursuers. As they came up within hailing distance, we ordered them to halt, which they declined by whirling their horses and burning the earth getting away. We threw a few rounds of lead after them, but they cut all desire for our acquaintance right there.

"We reached the river at a nearer point than the one at which we had entered, and crossed to the Texas side early the next morning. We missed a good ford by two miles and swam the river. At this ford was stationed a squad of regulars, and we turned our prizes over within an hour after crossing. We took a receipt for the men, stock, and equipments, and when we turned it over to our captain a week afterwards, we got the riot act read to us right. I noticed, however, the first time there was a division of prize money, one item was for the capture of four deserters."

"I don't reckon that captain had any scruples about taking his share of the prize money, did he?" inquired Gotch.

"No, I never knew anything like that to happen since I've been in the service."

"There used to be a captain in one of the upper country companies that held religious services in his company, and the boys claimed that he was equally good on a prayer, a fight, or holding aces in a poker game," said Gotch, as he filled his pipe.

Amongst Dad's other accomplishments was his unfailing readiness to tell of his experiences in the service. So after he had looked over the camp in general, he joined the group of lounging smokers and told us of an Indian fight in which he had participated.

"I can't imagine how this comes to be called Comanche Ford," said Dad. "Now the Comanches crossed over into the Panhandle country annually for the purpose of killing buffalo. For diversion and pastime, they were always willing to add horse-stealing and the murdering of settlers as a variation. They used to come over in big bands to hunt, and when ready to go back to their reservation in the Indian Territory, they would send the squaws on ahead, while the bucks would split into small bands and steal all the good horses in sight.

"Our old company was ordered out on the border once, when the Comanches were known to be south of Red River killing buffalo. This meant that on their return it would be advisable to look out for your horses or they would be missing. In order to cover as much territory as possible, the company was cut in three detachments. Our squad had twenty men in it under a lieutenant. We were patrolling a country known as the Tallow Cache Hills, glades and black-jack cross timbers alternating. All kinds of rumors of Indian depredations were reaching us almost daily, yet so far we had failed to locate or see an Indian.

"One day at noon we packed up and were going to move our camp farther west, when a scout, who had gone on ahead, rushed back with the news that he had sighted a band of Indians with quite a herd of horses pushing north. We led our pack mules, and keeping the shelter of the timber started to cut them off in their course. When we first sighted them, they were just crossing a glade, and the last buck had just left the timber. He had in his mouth an arrow shaft, which he was turning between his teeth to remove the sap. All had guns. The first warning the Indians received of our presence was a shot made by one of the men at this rear Indian. He rolled off his horse like a stone, and the next morning when we came back over their trail, he had that unfinished arrow in a death grip between his teeth. That first shot let the cat out, and we went after them.

" We had two big piebald calico mules, and when we charged those Indians, those pack mules outran every saddle horse which we had, and dashing into their horse herd, scattered them like partridges. Nearly every buck was riding a stolen horse, and for some cause they could n't get any speed out of them. We just rode all around them. There proved to be twenty-two Indians in the band, and one of them was a squaw. She was killed by accident.

"The chase had covered about two miles, when the horse she was riding fell from a shot by some of our crowd. The squaw recovered herself and came to her feet in time to see several carbines in the act of being leveled at her by our men. She instantly threw open the slight covering about her shoulders and revealed her sex. Some one called out not to shoot, that it was a squaw, and the carbines were lowered. As this squad passed on, she turned and ran for the protection of the nearest timber, and a second squad coming up and seeing the fleeing Indian, fired on her, killing her instantly. She had done the very thing she should not have done.

"It was a running fight from start to finish. We got the last one in the band about seven miles from the first one. The last one to fall was mounted on a fine horse, and if he had only ridden intelligently, he ought to have escaped. The funny thing about it was he was overtaken by the dullest, sleepiest horse in our command. The shooting and smell of powder must have put iron into him, for he died a hero. When this last Indian saw that he was going to be overtaken, his own horse being recently wounded, he hung on one side of the animal and returned the fire. At a range of ten yards he planted a bullet squarely in the leader's forehead, his own horse falling at the same instant. Those two horses fell dead so near that you could have tied their tails together. Our man was thrown so suddenly, that he came to his feet dazed, his eyes filled with dirt. The Indian stood not twenty steps away and fired several shots at him. Our man, in his blindness, stood there and beat the air with his gun, expecting the Indian to rush on him every moment. Had the buck used his gun for a club, it might have been different, but as long as he kept shooting, his enemy was safe. Half a dozen of us, who were near enough to witness his final fight, dashed up, and the Indian fell riddled with bullets.

"We went into camp after the fight was over with two wounded men and half a dozen dead or disabled horses. Those of us who had mounts in good fix scoured back and gathered in our packs and all the Indian and stolen horses that were unwounded. It looked like a butchery, but our minds were greatly relieved on that point the next day, when we found among their effects over a dozen fresh, bloody scalps, mostly women and children. There's times and circumstances in this service that make the toughest of us gloomy."

"How long ago was that?" inquired Orchard.

"Quite a while ago," replied Dad. "I ought to be able to tell exactly. I was a youngster then. Well, I'll tell you; it was during the reconstruction days, when Davis was governor. Figure it out yourself."

"Speaking of the disagreeable side of this

service," said Happy Jack, "reminds me of an incident that took all the nerve out of every one connected with it. When I first went into the service, there was a well-known horse-thief and smuggler down on the river, known as El Lobo. He operated on both sides of the Rio Grande, but generally stole his horses from the Texas side. He was a night owl. It was nothing for him to be seen at some ranch in the evening, and the next morning be met seventy-five or eighty miles distant. He was a good judge of horse-flesh, and never stole any but the best. His market was well in the interior of Mexico, and he supplied it liberally. He was a typical dandy, and like a sailor had a wife in every port. That was his weak point, and there's where we attacked him.

"He had made all kinds of fun of this service, and we concluded to have him at any cost. Accordingly we located his women and worked on them. Mexican beauty is always over-rated, but one of his conquests in that line came as near being the ideal for a rustic beauty as that nationality produces. This girl was about twenty, and lived with a questionable mother at a ranchito back from the river about thirty miles. In form and feature there was nothing lacking, while the smouldering fire of her black eyes would win saint or thief alike.

Born in poverty and ignorance, she was a child of circumstance, and fell an easy victim to El Lobo, who lavished every attention upon her. There was no present too costly for him, and on his periodical visits he dazzled her with gifts. But infatuations of that class generally have an end, often a sad one.

" We had a half-blood in our company, who was used as a rival to El Lobo in gathering any information that might be afloat, and at the same time, when opportunity offered, in sowing the wormwood of jealousy. This was easy, for we collected every item in the form of presents he ever made her rival señoritas. When these forces were working, our half-blood pushed his claims for recognition. Our wages and prize money were at his disposal, and in time they won. The neglect shown her by El Lobo finally turned her against him, apparently, and she agreed to betray his whereabouts the first opportunity — on one condition. And that was, that if we succeeded in capturing him, we were to bring him before her, that she might, in his helplessness, taunt him for his perfidy towards her. We were willing to make any concession to get him, so this request was readily granted.

" The deserted condition of the ranchito where the girl lived was to our advantage as well as his. The few families that dwelt there had their flocks to look after, and the coming or going of a passer-by was scarcely noticed. Our man on his visits carefully concealed the fact that he was connected with this service, for El Lobo's lavish use of money made him friends wherever he went, and afforded him all the seclusion he needed.

" It was over a month before the wolf made his appearance, and we were informed of the fact. He stayed at an outside pastor's camp, visiting the ranch only after dark. A corral was mentioned, where within a few days' time, at the farthest, he would pen a bunch of saddle horses. There had once been wells at this branding pen, but on their failing to furnish water continuously they had been abandoned. El Lobo had friends at his command to assist him in securing the best horses in the country. So accordingly we planned to pay our respects to him at these deserted wells.

" The second night of our watch, we were rewarded by having three men drive into these corrals about twenty saddle horses. They had barely time to tie their mounts outside and enter the pen, when four of us slipped in behind them and changed the programme a trifle. El Lobo was one of the men. He was very polite and nice, but that did n't prevent us from ironing him securely, as we did his companions also.

" It was almost midnight when we reached the ranchito where the girl lived. We asked him if he had any friends at this ranch whom he wished to see. This he denied. When we informed him that by special request a lady wished to bid him farewell, he lost some of his bluster and bravado. We all dismounted, leaving one man outside with the other two prisoners, and entered a small yard where the girl lived. Our half-blood aroused her and called her out to meet her friend, El Lobo. The girl delayed us some minutes, and we apologized to him for the necessity of irons and our presence in meeting his Dulce Corazon. When the girl came out we were some distance from the jacal. There was just moonlight enough to make her look beautiful.

"As she advanced, she called him by some pet name in their language, when he answered her gruffly, accusing her of treachery, and turned his back upon her. She approached within a few feet, when it was noticeable that she was racked with emotion, and asked him if he had no kind word for her. Turning on her, he repeated the accusation of treachery, and applied a vile expression to her. That moment the girl flashed into a fiend, and throwing a shawl from her shoulders, revealed a pistol, firing it twice before a man could stop her. El Lobo sank in his tracks, and she begged us to let her trample his lifeless body. Later, when composed, she told us that we had not used her any more than she had used us, in bringing him helpless to her. As things turned out it looked that way.

" We lashed the dead thief on his horse and rode until daybreak, when we buried him. We could have gotten a big reward for him dead or alive, and we had the evidence of his death, but the manner in which we got it made it undesirable. El Lobo was missed, but the manner of his going was a secret of four men and a Mexican girl. The other two prisoners went over the road, and we even reported to them that he had attempted to strangle her, and we shot him to save her. Something had to be said."

The smoking and yarning had ended. Darkness had settled over the camp but a short while, when every one was sound asleep. It must have been near midnight when a number of us were aroused by the same disturbance. The boys sat bolt upright and listened eagerly. We were used to being awakened by shots, and the cause of our sudden awakening was believed to be the same, — a shot.

While the exchange of opinion was going the round, all anxiety on that point was dispelled by a second shot, the flash of which could be distinctly seen across the river below the ford.

As Dad stood up and answered it with a shrill whistle, every man reached for his carbine and flattened himself out on the ground. The whistle was answered, and shortly the splash of quite a cavalcade could be heard fording the river. Several times they halted, our fire having died out, and whistles were exchanged between them and Root. When they came within fifty yards of camp and their outlines could be distinguished against the sky line in the darkness, they were ordered to halt, and a dozen carbines clicked an accompaniment to the order.

"Who are you?" demanded Root.

"A detachment from Company M, Texas Rangers," was the reply.

"If you are Rangers, give us a maxim of the service," said Dad.

"*Don't wait for the other man to shoot first*," came the response.

"Ride in, that passes here," was Dad's greeting and welcome.

They were a detachment of fifteen men, and had ridden from the Pecos on the south, nearly the same distance which we had come.

They had similar orders to ours, but were advised that they would meet our detachment at this ford. In less than an hour every man was asleep again, and quiet reigned in the Ranger camp at Comanche Ford on the Concho.

IX

AROUND THE SPADE WAGON

IT was an early spring. The round-up was set for the 10th of June. The grass was well forward, while the cattle had changed their shaggy winter coats to glossy suits of summer silk. The brands were as readable as an alphabet.

It was one day yet before the round-up of the Cherokee Strip. This strip of leased Indian lands was to be worked in three divisions. We were on our way to represent the Coldwater Pool in the western division, on the annual round-up. Our outfit was four men and thirty horses. We were to represent a range that had twelve thousand cattle on it, a total of forty-seven brands. We had been in the saddle since early morning, and as we came out on a narrow divide, we caught our first glimpse of the Cottonwoods at Antelope Springs, the rendezvous for this division. The setting sun was scarcely half an hour high, and the camp was yet five miles distant. We had covered sixty miles that day, traveling light, our bedding lashed on gentle saddle horses. We rode up the mesa quite a little distance to avoid some rough broken country, then turned southward toward the Springs. Before turning off, we could see with the naked eye signs of life at the meeting-point. The wagon sheets of half a dozen chuck-wagons shone white in the dim distance, while small bands of saddle horses could be distinctly seen grazing about.

When we halted at noon that day to change our mounts, we sighted to the northward some seven miles distant an outfit similar to our own. We were on the lookout for this cavalcade; they were supposed to be the "Spade" outfit, on their way to attend the round-up in the middle division, where our pasture lay. This year, as in years past, we had exchanged the courtesies of the range with them. Their men on our division were made welcome at our wagon, and we on theirs were extended the same courtesy. For this reason we had hoped to meet them and exchange the chronicle of the day, concerning the condition of cattle on their range, the winter drift, and who would be captain this year on the western division, but had traveled the entire day without meeting a man.

Night had almost set in when we reached the camp, and to our satisfaction and delight found the Spade wagon already there, though their men and horses would not arrive until the next day. To hungry men like ourselves, the welcome of their cook was hospitality in the fullest sense of the word. We stretched ropes from the wagon wheels, and in a few moments' time were busy hobbling our mounts. Darkness had settled over the camp as we were at this work, while an occasional horseman rode by with the common inquiry, "Whose outfit is this?" and the cook, with one end of the rope in his hand, would feel the host in him sufficiently to reply in tones supercilious, "The Coldwater Pool men are with us this year."

Our arrival was heralded through the camp with the same rapidity with which gossip circulates, equally in a tenement alley or the upper crust of society. The cook had informed us that we had been inquired for by some Panhandle man; so before we had finished hobbling, a stranger sang out across the ropes in the darkness, "Is Billy Edwards here?" Receiving an affirmative answer from among the horses' feet, he added, "Come out, then, and shake hands with a friend."

Edwards arose from his work, and looking across the backs of the circle of horses about him, at the undistinguishable figure at the rope, replied, "Whoever you are, I reckon the acquaintance will hold good until I get these horses hobbled."

"Who is it?" inquired "Mouse" from over near the hind wheel of the wagon, where he was applying the hemp to the horses' ankles.

"I don't know," said Billy, as he knelt among the horses and resumed his work,— "some geranium out there wants me to come out and shake hands, pow-wow, and make some medicine with him; that's all. Say, we'll leave Chino for picket, and that Chihuahua cutting horse of Coon's, you have to put a rope on when you come to him. He's too touchy to sabe hobbles if you don't."

When we had finished hobbling, and the horses were turned loose, the stranger proved to be "Babe" Bradshaw, an old chum of Edwards's. The Spade cook added an earthly laurel to his temporal crown with the supper to which he shortly invited us. Bradshaw had eaten with the general wagon, but he sat around while we ate. There was little conversation during the supper, for our appetites were such and the spread so inviting that it simply absorbed us.

"Don't bother me," said Edwards to his old chum, in reply to some inquiry. "Can't you see that I'm occupied at present?"

We did justice to the supper, having had no
dinner that day. The cook even urged, with
an earnestness worthy of a motherly landlady,
several dishes, but his browned potatoes and
roast beef claimed our attention. "Well, what
are you doing in this country anyhow?" inquired Edwards of Bradshaw, when the inner
man had been thoroughly satisfied.

"Well, sir, I have a document in my pocket,
with sealing wax but no ribbons on it, which
says that I am the duly authorized representative of the Panhandle Cattle Association. I
also have a book in my pocket showing every
brand and the names of its owners, and there is
a whole raft of them. I may go to St. Louis
to act as inspector for my people when the
round-up ends."

"You're just as windy as ever, Babe," said
Billy. "Strange I did n't recognize you when
you first spoke. You're getting natural now,
though. I suppose you're borrowing horses,
like all these special inspectors do. It's all
right with me, but good men must be scarce
in your section or you've improved rapidly
since you left us. By the way, there is a man
or four lying around here that also represents
about forty-seven brands. Possibly you'd better not cut any of their cattle or you might
get them cut back on you."

"Do you remember," said Babe, "when I dissolved with the 'Ohio' outfit and bought in with the 'LX' people?"

"When you what?" repeated Edwards.

"Well, then, when I was discharged by the 'Ohio's' and got a job ploughing fire-guards with the 'LX's.' Is that plain enough for your conception? I learned a lesson then that has served me since to good advantage. Don't hesitate to ask for the best job on the works, for if you don't you 'll see some one get it that is n't as well qualified to fill it as you are. So if you happen to be in St. Louis, call around and see me at the Panhandle headquarters. Don't send in any card by a nigger; walk right in. I might give you some other pointers, but you could n't appreciate them. You 'll more than likely be driving a chuck-wagon in a few years."

These old cronies from boyhood sparred along in give-and-take repartee for some time, finally drifting back to boyhood days, while the harshness that pervaded their conversation before became mild and genial.

"Have you ever been back in old San Saba since we left?" inquired Edwards after a long meditative silence.

"Oh, yes, I spent a winter back there two years ago, though it was hard lines to enjoy yourself. I managed to romance about for two or three months, sowing turnip seed and teaching dancing-school. The girls that you and I knew are nearly all married."

"What ever became of the O'Shea girls?" asked Edwards. "You know that I was high card once with the eldest."

"You 'd better comfort yourself with the thought," answered Babe, "for you could n't play third fiddle in her string now. You remember old Dennis O'Shea was land-poor all his life. Well, in the land and cattle boom a few years ago he was picked up and set on a pedestal. It 's wonderful what money can do! The old man was just common bog Irish all his life, until a cattle syndicate bought his lands and cattle for twice what they were worth. Then he blossomed into a capitalist. He always was a trifle hide-bound. Get all you can and can all you get, took precedence and became the first law with your papa-in-law. The old man used to say that the prettiest sight he ever saw was the smoke arising from a 'Snake' branding-iron. They moved to town, and have been to Europe since they left the ranch. Jed Lynch, you know, was smitten on the youngest girl. Well, he had the nerve to call on them after their return from Europe. He says that they live in a big house, their name's on the door, and you have to ring a bell, and then a nigger meets you. It must make a man feel awkward to live around a wagon all his days, and then suddenly change to style and put on a heap of dog. Jed says the red-headed girl, the middle one, married some fellow, and they live with the old folks. He says the other girls treated him nicely, but the old lady, she has got it bad. He says that she just languishes on a sofa, cuts into the conversation now and then, and simply swells up. She don't let the old man come into the parlor at all. Jed says that when the girls were describing their trip through Europe, one of them happened to mention Rome, when the old lady interrupted: 'Rome? Rome? Let me see, I've forgotten, girls. Where is Rome?'

" 'Don't you remember when we were in Italy,' said one of the girls, trying to refresh her memory.

" 'Oh, yes, now I remember; that's where I bought you girls such nice long red stockings.'

"The girls suddenly remembered some duty about the house that required their immediate attention, and Jed says that he looked out of the window."

" So you think I've lost my number, do you?" commented Edwards, as he lay on his back and fondly patted a comfortable stomach.

"Well, possibly I have, but it's some consolation to remember that that very good woman that you're slandering used to give me the glad hand and cut the pie large when I called. I may be out of the game, but I'd take a chance yet if I were present; that's what!"

They were singing over at one of the wagons across the draw, and after the song ended, Bradshaw asked, "What ever became of Raneka Bill Hunter?"

"Oh, he's drifting about," said Edwards. "Mouse here can tell you about him. They're old college chums."

"Raneka was working for the '–B Q' people last summer," said Mouse, "but was discharged for hanging a horse, or rather he discharged himself. It seems that some one took a fancy to a horse in his mount. The last man to buy into an outfit that way always gets all the bad horses for his string. As Raneka was a new man there, the result was that some excuse was given him to change, and they rung in a spoilt horse on him in changing. Being new that way, he was n't on to the horses. The first time he tried to saddle this new horse he showed up bad. The horse trotted up to him when the rope fell on his neck, reared up nicely and playfully, and threw out his forefeet, stripping the three upper buttons off

Bill's vest pattern. Bill never said a word about his intentions, but tied him to the corral fence and saddled up his own private horse. There were several men around camp, but they said nothing, being a party to the deal, though they noticed Bill riding away with the spoilt horse. He took him down on the creek about a mile from camp and hung him.

"How did he do it? Why, there was a big cottonwood grew on a bluff bank of the creek. One limb hung out over the bluff, over the bed of the creek. He left the running noose on the horse's neck, climbed out on this over-hanging limb, taking the rope through a fork directly over the water. He then climbed down and snubbed the free end of the rope to a small tree, and began taking in his slack. When the rope began to choke the horse, he reared and plunged, throwing himself over the bluff. That settled his ever hurting any one. He was hung higher than Haman. Bill never went back to the camp, but struck out for other quarters. There was a month's wages coming to him, but he would get that later or they might keep it. Life had charms for an old-timer like Bill, and he did n't hanker for any reputation as a broncho-buster. It generally takes a verdant to pine for such honors.

"Last winter when Bill was riding the

chuck line, he ran up against a new experience. It seems that some newcomer bought a range over on Black Bear. This new man sought to set at defiance the customs of the range. It was currently reported that he had refused to invite people to stay for dinner, and preferred that no one would ask for a night's lodging, even in winter. This was the gossip of the camps for miles around, so Bill and some juniper of a pardner thought they would make a call on him and see how it was. They made it a point to reach his camp shortly after noon. They met the owner just coming out of the dug-out as they rode up. They exchanged the compliments of the hour, when the new man turned and locked the door of the dug-out with a padlock. Bill sparred around the main question, but finally asked if it was too late to get dinner, and was very politely informed that dinner was over. This latter information was, however, qualified with a profusion of regrets. After a confession of a hard ride made that morning from a camp many miles distant, Bill asked the chance to remain over night. Again the travelers were met with serious regrets, as no one would be at camp that night, business calling the owner away; he was just starting then. The cowman led out his horse, and after mounting and expressing for the last time his sincere regrets that he could not extend to them the hospitalities of his camp, rode away.

"Bill and his pardner moseyed in an opposite direction a short distance and held a parley. Bill was so nonplussed at the reception that it took him some little time to collect his thoughts. When it thoroughly dawned on him that the courtesies of the range had been trampled under foot by a rank newcomer and himself snubbed, he was aroused to action.

"'Let's go back,' said Bill to his pardner, 'and at least leave our card. He might not like it if we did n't.'

"They went back and dismounted about ten steps from the door. They shot every cartridge they both had, over a hundred between them, through the door, fastened a card with their correct names on it, and rode away. One of the boys that was working there, but was absent at the time, says there was a number of canned tomato and corn crates ranked up at the rear of the dug-out, in range with the door. This lad says that it looked as if they had a special grievance against those canned goods, for they were riddled with lead. That fellow lost enough by that act to have fed all the chuck-line men that would bother him in a year.

" Raneka made it a rule," continued Mouse,
" to go down and visit the Cheyennes every
winter, sometimes staying a month. He could
make a good stagger at speaking their tongue,
so that together with his knowledge of the
Spanish and the sign language he could con-
verse with them readily. He was perfectly
at home with them, and they all liked him.
When he used to let his hair grow long, he
looked like an Indian. Once, when he was
wrangling horses for us during the beef-shipping season, we passed him off for an Indian
on some dining-room girls. George Wall was
working with us that year, and had gone in
ahead to see about the cars and find out when
we could pen and the like. We had to drive
to the State line, then, to ship. George took
dinner at the best hotel in the town, and asked
one of the dining-room girls if he might bring
in an Indian to supper the next evening. They
did n't know, so they referred him to the land-
lord. George explained to that auger, who, not
wishing to offend us, consented. There were
about ten girls in the dining-room, and they
were on the lookout for the Indian. The next
night we penned a little before dark. Not a
man would eat at the wagon; every one rode
for the hotel. We fixed Bill up in fine shape,
put feathers in his hair, streaked his face with

red and yellow, and had him all togged out in buckskin, even to moccasins. As we entered the dining-room, George led him by the hand, assuring all the girls that he was perfectly harmless. One long table accommodated us all. George, who sat at the head with our Indian on his right, begged the girls not to act as though they were afraid ; he might notice it. Wall fed him pickles and lump sugar until the supper was brought on. Then he pushed back his chair about four feet, and stared at the girls like an idiot. When George ordered him to eat, he stood up at the table. When he would n't let him stand, he took the plate on his knee, and ate one side dish at a time. Finally, when he had eaten everything that suited his taste, he stood up and signed with his hands to the group of girls, muttering, 'Wo-haw, wo-haw.'

" 'He wants some more beef,' said Wall. 'Bring him some more beef.' After a while he stood up and signed again, George interpreting his wants to the dining-room girls: 'Bring him some coffee. He 's awful fond of coffee.'

"That supper lasted an hour, and he ate enough to kill a horse. As we left the dining-room, he tried to carry away a sugar-bowl, but Wall took it away from him. As we passed out George turned back and apologized to the girls, saying, 'He's a good Injun. I promised him he might eat with us. He 'll talk about this for months now. When he goes back to his tribe he 'll tell his squaws all about you girls feeding him.'"

"Seems like I remember that fellow Wall," said Bradshaw, meditating.

"Why, of course you do. Were n't you with us when we voted the bonds to the railroad company?" asked Edwards.

"No, never heard of it; must have been after I left. What business did you have voting bonds ?"

"Tell him, Coon. I 'm too full for utterance," said Edwards.

"If you 'd been in this country you 'd heard of it," said Coon Floyd. "For a few years everything was dated from that event. It was like 'when the stars fell,' and the 'surrender' with the old-time darkies at home. It seems that some new line of railroad wanted to build in, and wanted bonds voted to them as bonus. Some foxy agent for this new line got among the long-horns, who own the cattle on this Strip, and showed them that it was to their interests to get a competing line in the cattle traffic. The result was, these old long-horns got owly, laid their heads together, and made a little medicine. Every mother's son of us in the Strip was entitled to claim a home somewhere, so they put it up that we should come in and vote for the bonds. It was believed it would be a close race if they carried, for it was by counties that the bonds were voted. Towns that the road would run through would vote unanimously for them, but outlying towns would vote solidly against the bonds. There was a big lot of money used, wherever it came from, for we were royally entertained. Two or three days before the date set for the election, they began to head for this cow-town, every man on his top horse. Everything was as free as air, and we all understood that a new railroad was a good thing for the cattle interests. We gave it not only our votes, but moral support likewise.

"It was a great gathering. The hotels fed us, and the liveries cared for our horses. The liquid refreshments were provided by the prohibition druggists of the town and were as free as the sunlight. There was an underestimate made on the amount of liquids required, for the town was dry about thirty minutes; but a regular train was run through from Wichita ahead of time, and the embarrassment overcome. There was an opposition line of railroad working against the bonds, but they did n't have any better sense than to send a man down to our town to counteract our exertions. Public sentiment was a delicate matter with us, and while this man had no influence with any of us, we did n't feel the same toward him as we might. He was distributing his tickets around, and putting up a good argument, possibly, from his point of view, when some of these old long-horns hinted to the boys to show the fellow that he was n't wanted. 'Don't hurt him,' said one old cow-man to this same Wall, 'but give him a scare, so he will know that we don't indorse him a little bit. Let him know that this town knows how to vote without being told. I 'll send a man to rescue him, when things have gone far enough. You 'll know when to let up.'

"That was sufficient. George went into a store and cut off about fifty feet of new rope. Some fellows that knew how tied a hangman's knot. As we came up to the stranger, we heard him say to a man, 'I tell you, sir, these bonds will pauperize unborn gener—' But the noose dropped over his neck, and cut short his argument. We led him a block and a half through the little town, during which there was a pointed argument between Wall and a " Z— " man whether the city scales or the stockyards arch gate would be the best place to hang him. There were a hundred men around him and hanging on to the rope, when a druggist, whom most of them knew, burst through the crowd, and whipping out a knife cut the rope within a few feet of his neck. 'What in hell are you varments trying to do?' roared the druggist. 'This man is a cousin of mine. Going to hang him, are you? Well, you'll have to hang me with him when you do.'

"'Just as soon make it two as one,' snarled George. 'When did you get the chips in this game, I'd like to know? Oppose the progress of the town, too, do you?'

"'No, I don't,' said the druggist, 'and I'll see that my cousin here does n't.'

"'That's all we ask, then,' said Wall; 'turn him loose, boys. We don't want to hang no man. We hold you responsible if he opens his mouth again against the bonds.'

"'Hold me responsible, gentlemen,' said the druggist, with a profound bow. 'Come with me, Cousin,' he said to the Anti.

"The druggist took him through his store, and up some back stairs; and once he had him alone, this was his advice, as reported to us later: 'You're a stranger to me. I lied to those men, but I saved your life. Now, I'll take you to the four-o'clock train, and get you out of this town. By this act I'll incur the hatred of these people that I live amongst. So you let the idea go out that you are my cousin. Sabe? Now, stay right here and I'll bring you anything you want, but for Heaven's sake, don't give me away.'

"'Is—is—is the four o'clock train the first out?' inquired the new cousin.

"'It is the first. I'll see you through this. I'll come up and see you every hour. Take things cool and easy now. I'm your friend, remember,' was the comfort they parted on.

"There were over seven hundred votes cast, and only one against the bonds. How that one vote got in is yet a mystery. There were no hard drinkers among the boys, all easy drinkers, men that never refused to drink. Yet voting was a little new to them, and possibly that was how this mistake occurred. We got the returns early in the evening. The county had gone by a handsome majority for the bonds. The committee on entertainment had provided a ball for us in the basement of the Opera House, it being the largest room in town. When the good news began to circulate, the merchants began building bonfires. Fellows who did n't have extra togs on for the ball got out their horses, and in squads of twenty to fifty rode through the town, painting her red. If there was one shot fired that night, there were ten thousand.

"I bought a white shirt and went to the ball. To show you how general the good feeling amongst everybody was, I squeezed the hand of an alfalfa widow during a waltz, who instantly reported the affront offered to her gallant. In her presence he took me to task for the offense. 'Young man,' said the doctor, with a quiet wink, 'this lady is under my protection. The fourteenth amendment don't apply to you nor me. Six-shooters, however, make us equal. Are you armed?'

"'I am, sir.'

"'Unfortunately, I am not. Will you kindly excuse me, say ten minutes?'

"'Certainly, sir, with pleasure.'

"'There are ladies present,' he observed. 'Let us retire.'

"On my consenting, he turned to the offended dame, and in spite of her protests and appeals to drop matters, we left the ballroom, glaring daggers at each other. Once outside, he slapped me on the back, and said, 'Say, we'll just have time to run up to my office, where I have some choice old copper-distilled, sent me by a very dear friend in Kentucky.'

"The goods were all he claimed for them,

and on our return he asked me as a personal favor to apologize to the lady, admitting that he was none too solid with her himself. My doing so, he argued, would fortify him with her and wipe out rivals. The doctor was a rattling good fellow, and I'd even taken off my new shirt for him, if he'd said the word. When I made the apology, I did it on the grounds that I could not afford to have any difference, especially with a gentleman who would willingly risk his life for a lady who claimed his protection.

"No, if you never heard of voting the bonds you certainly have n't kept very close tab on affairs in this Strip. Two or three men whom I know refused to go in and vote. They ain't working in this country now. It took some of the boys ten days to go and come, but there was n't a word said. Wages went on just the same. You ain't asleep, are you, Don Guillermo?"

"Oh, no," said Edwards, with a yawn, "I feel just like the nigger did when he eat his fill of possum, corn bread, and new molasses: pushed the platter away and said, 'Go way, 'lasses, you done los' yo' sweetness.'"

Bradshaw made several attempts to go, but each time some thought would enter his mind and he would return with questions about former acquaintances. Finally he inquired, "What ever became of that little fellow who was sick about your camp?"

Edwards meditated until Mouse said, "He's thinking about little St. John, the fiddler."

"Oh, yes, Patsy St. John, the little glass-blower," said Edwards, as he sat up on a roll of bedding. "He's dead long ago. Died at our camp. I did something for him that I've often wondered who would do the same for me — I closed his eyes when he died. You know he came to us with the mark on his brow. There was no escape; he had consumption. He wanted to live, and struggled hard to avoid going. Until three days before his death he was hopeful; always would tell us how much better he was getting, and every one could see that he was gradually going. We always gave him gentle horses to ride, and he would go with us on trips that we were afraid would be his last. There was n't a man on the range who ever said 'No' to him. He was one of those little men you can't help but like; small physically, but with a heart as big as an ox's. He lived about three years on the range, was welcome wherever he went, and never made an enemy or lost a friend. He could n't; it was n't in him. I don't remember now how he came to the range, but think he was advised by doctors to lead an outdoor life for a change.

"He was born in the South, and was a glass-blower by occupation. He would have died sooner, but for his pluck and confidence that he would get well. He changed his mind one morning, lost hope that he would ever get well, and died in three days. It was in the spring. We were going out one morning to put in a flood-gate on the river, which had washed away in a freshet. He was ready to go along. He had n't been on a horse in two weeks. No one ever pretended to notice that he was sick. He was sensitive if you offered any sympathy, so no one offered to assist, except to saddle his horse. The old horse stood like a kitten. Not a man pretended to notice, but we all saw him put his foot in the stir-rup three different times and attempt to lift himself into the saddle. He simply lacked the strength. He asked one of the boys to un-saddle the horse, saying he would n't go with us. Some of the boys suggested that it was a long ride, and it was best he did n't go, that we would hardly get back until after dark. But we had no idea that he was so near his end. After we left, he went back to the shack and told the cook he had changed his mind,

— that he was going to die. That night, when we came back, he was lying on his cot. We all tried to jolly him, but each got the same answer from him, 'I'm going to die.' The outfit to a man was broke up about it, but all kept up a good front. We tried to make him believe it was only one of his bad days, but he knew otherwise. He asked Joe Box and Ham Rhodes, the two biggest men in the outfit, six-footers and an inch each, to sit one on each side of his cot until he went to sleep. He knew better than any of us how near he was to crossing. But it seemed he felt safe between these two giants. We kept up a running conversation in jest with one another, though it was empty mockery. But he never pretended to notice. It was plain to us all that the fear was on him. We kept near the shack the next day, some of the boys always with him. The third evening he seemed to rally, talked with us all, and asked if some of the boys would not play the fiddle. He was a good player himself. Several of the boys played old favorites of his, interspersed with stories and songs, until the evening was passing pleasantly. We were recovering from our despondency with this noticeable recovery on his part, when he whispered to his two big nurses to prop him up. They did so with pillows and parkers, and he actually smiled on us all. He whispered to Joe, who in turn asked the lad sitting on the foot of the cot to play 'Farewell, my Sunny Southern Home.' Strange we had forgotten that old air, — for it was a general favorite with us, — and stranger now that he should ask for it. As that old familiar air was wafted out from the instrument, he raised his eyes, and seemed to wander in his mind as if trying to follow the refrain. Then something came over him, for he sat up rigid, pointing out his hand at the empty space, and muttered, 'There stands — mother — now — under — the — oleanders. Who is — that with — her? Yes, I had — a sister. Open — the — windows. It — is — getting — dark — dark — dark.'

"Large hands laid him down tenderly, but a fit of coughing came on. He struggled in a hemorrhage for a moment, and then crossed over to the waiting figures among the oleanders. Of all the broke-up outfits, we were the most. Dead tough men bawled like babies. I had a good one myself. When we came around to our senses, we all admitted it was for the best. Since he could not get well, he was better off. We took him next day about ten miles and buried him with those freighters who were killed when the Pawnees raided this country. Some man will plant corn over their graves some day."

As Edwards finished his story, his voice trembled and there were tears in his eyes. A strange silence had come over those gathered about the camp-fire. Mouse, to conceal his emotion, pretended to be asleep, while Bradshaw made an effort to clear his throat of something that would neither go up nor down, and failing in this, turned and walked away without a word. Silently we unrolled the beds, and with saddles for pillows and the dome of heaven for a roof, we fell asleep.

X

THE RANSOM OF DON RAMON
MORA

ON the southern slope of the main tableland which divides the waters of the Nueces and Rio Grande rivers in Texas, lies the old Spanish land grant of "Agua Dulce," and the rancho by that name. Twice within the space of fifteen years was an appeal to the sword taken over the ownership of the territory between these rivers. Sparsely settled by the descendants of the original grantees, with an occasional American ranchman, it is to-day much the same as when the treaty of peace gave it to the stronger republic.

This frontier on the south has undergone few changes in the last half century, and no improvements have been made. Here the smuggler against both governments finds an inviting field. The bandit and the robber feel equally at home under either flag. Revolutionists hatch their plots against the powers that be; sedition takes on life and finds adherents eager to bear arms and apply the torch.

Within a dozen years of the close of the century just past, this territory was infested by a band of robbers, whose boldness has had few equals in the history of American brigandage. The Bedouins of the Orient justify their freebooting by accounting it a religious duty, looking upon every one against their faith as an Infidel, and therefore common property. These bandits could offer no such excuse, for they plundered people of their own faith and blood. They were Mexicans, a hybrid mixture of Spanish atrocity and Indian cruelty. They numbered from ten to twenty, and for several months terrorized the Mexican inhabitants on both sides of the river. On the American side they were particular never to molest any one except those of their own nationality. These they robbed with impunity, nor did their victims dare to complain to the authorities, so thoroughly were they terrified and coerced.

The last and most daring act of these marauders was the kidnapping of Don Ramon Mora, owner of the princely grant of Agua Dulce. Thousands of cattle and horses ranged over the vast acres of his ranch, and he was reputed to be a wealthy man. No one ever enjoyed the hospitality of Agua Dulce but went his way with an increased regard for its owner and his estimable Castilian family. The rancho lay back from the river probably sixty miles, and was on the border of the chaparral, which was the rendezvous of the robbers. Don Ramon had a pleasant home in one of the river towns. One June he and his family had gone to the ranch, intending to spend a few weeks there. He had notified cattle-buyers of this vacation, and had invited them to visit him there either on business or pleasure.

One evening an unknown vaquero rode up to the rancho and asked for Don Ramon. That gentleman presenting himself, the stranger made known his errand: a certain firm of well-known drovers, friends of the ranchero, were encamped for the night at a ranchita some ten miles distant. They regretted that they could not visit him, but they would be pleased to see him. They gave as an excuse for not calling that they were driving quite a herd of cattle, and the corrals at this little ranch were unsafe for the number they had, so that they were compelled to hold outside or night-herd. This very plausible story was accepted without question by Don Ramon, who well understood the handling of herds. Inviting the messenger to some refreshment, he ordered his horse saddled and made preparation to return with this pseudo vaquero. Telling his family that he would be gone for the night, he rode away with the stranger.

There were several thickety groves, extending from the main chaparral out for considerable distance on the prairie, but not of as rank a growth as on the alluvial river bottoms. These thickets were composed of thorny underbrush, frequently as large as fruit trees and of a density which made them impenetrable, except by those thoroughly familiar with the few established trails. The road from Agua Dulce to the ranchita was plain and well known, yet passing through several arms of the main body of the chaparral. Don Ramon and his guide reached one of these thickets after nightfall. Suddenly they were surrounded by a dozen horsemen, who, with oaths and jests, told him that he was their prisoner. Relieving Don Ramon of his firearms and other valuables, one of the bandits took the bridle off his horse, and putting a rope around the animal's neck, the band turned towards the river with their captive. Near morning they went into one of their many retreats in the chaparral, fettering their prisoner. What the feelings of Don Ramon Mora were that night is not for pen to picture, for they must have been indescribable.

The following day the leader of these bandits held several conversations with him, asking in regard to his family, his children in particular, their names, number, and ages. When evening came they set out once more southward, crossing the Rio Grande during the night at an unused ford. The next morning found them well inland on the Mexican side, and encamped in one of their many chaparral rendezvous. Here they spent several days, sometimes, however, only a few of the band being present. The density of the thickets on the first and second bottoms of this river, extending back inland often fifty miles, made this camp and refuge almost inaccessible. The country furnished their main subsistence; fresh meat was always at hand, while their comrades, scouting the river towns, supplied such comforts as were lacking.

Don Ramon's appeals to his captors to know his offense and what his punishment was to be were laughed at until he had been their prisoner a week. One night several of the party returned, awoke him out of a friendly sleep, and he was notified that their chief would join them by daybreak, and then he would know what his offense had been. When this personage made his appearance, he ordered Don Ramon released from his fetters. Every one in camp showed obeisance to him. After holding a general conversation with his followers, he approached Don Ramon, the band forming a circle about the prisoner and their chief.

"Don Ramon Mora," he began, with mock courtesy, "doubtless you consider yourself an innocent and abused person. In that you are wrong. Your offense is a political one. Your family for three generations have opposed the freedom of Mexico. When our people were conquered and control was given to the French, it was through the treachery of such men as you. Treason is unpardonable, Señor Mora. It is useless to enumerate your crimes against human liberty. Living as you do under a friendly government, you have incited the ignorant to revolution and revolt against the native rulers. Secret agents of our common country have shadowed you for years. It is useless to deny your guilt. Your execution, therefore, will be secret, in order that your co-workers in infamy shall not take alarm, but may meet a similar fate."

Turning to one of the party who had acted as leader at the time of his capture, he gave these instructions: "Be in no hurry to execute these orders. Death is far too light a sentence to fit his crime. He is beyond a full measure of justice." There was a chorus of "bravos" when the bandit chief finished this trumped-up charge. As he turned from the prisoner, Don Ramon pleadingly begged, "Only take me before an established court that I may prove my innocence."

"No! sentence has been passed upon you. If you hope for mercy, it must come from there," and the chief pointed heavenward. One of the band led out the arch-chief's horse, and with a parting instruction to "conceal his grave carefully," he rode away with but a single attendant.

As they led Don Ramon back to his blanket and replaced the fetters, his cup of sorrow was full to overflowing. Oddly enough the leader, since sentence of death had been pronounced upon his victim, was the only one of the band who showed any kindness. The others were brutal in their jeers and taunts. Some remarks burned into his sensitive nature as vitriol burns into metal. The bandit leader alone offered little kindnesses.

Two days later, the acting chief ordered the irons taken from the captive's feet, and the two men, with but a single attendant, who kept a respectful distance, started out for a stroll. The bandit chief expressed his regret at the sad duty which had been allotted him, and assured Don Ramon that he would gladly make his time as long as was permissible.

" I thank you for your kindness," said Don Ramon, " but is there no chance to be given me to prove the falsity of these charges? Am I condemned to die without a hearing? "

" There is no hope from that source."

" Is there any hope from any source? "

" Scarcely," replied the leader, "and still, if we could satisfy those in authority over us that you had been executed as ordered, and if my men could be bribed to certify the fact if necessary, and if you pledge us to quit the country forever, who would know to the contrary? True, our lives would be in jeopardy, and it would mean death to you if you betrayed us."

" Is this possible? " asked Don Ramon excitedly.

" The color of gold makes a good many things possible."

" I would gladly give all I possess in the world for one hour's peace in the presence of my family, even if in the next my soul was summoned to the bar of God. True, in lands and cattle I am wealthy, but the money at my command is limited, though I wish it were otherwise."

" It is a fortunate thing that you are a man

of means. Say nothing to your guards, and I will have a talk this very night with two men whom I can trust, and we will see what can be done for you. Come, señor, don't despair, for I feel there is some hope," concluded the bandit.

The family of Don Ramon were uneasy but not alarmed by his failure to return to them the day following his departure. After two days had passed, during which no word had come from him, his wife sent an old servant to see if he was still at the ranchita. There the man learned that his master had not been seen, nor had there been any drovers there recently. Under the promise of secrecy, the servant was further informed that, on the very day that Don Ramon had left his home, a band of robbers had driven into a corral at a ranch in the *monte* a remudo of ranch horses, and, asking no one's consent, had proceeded to change their mounts, leaving their own tired horses. This they did at noonday, without so much as a hand raised in protest, so terrified were the people of the ranch.

On the servant's return to Agua Dulce, the alarm and grief of the family were pitiful, as was their helplessness. When darkness set in Señora Mora sent a letter by a peon to an old family friend at his home on the river.

The next night three men, for mutual protection, brought back a reply. From it these plausible deductions were made: —

That Don Ramon had been kidnapped for a ransom; that these bandits no doubt were desperate men who would let nothing interfere with their plans; that to notify the authorities and ask for help might end in his murder; and that if kidnapped for a ransom, overtures for his redemption would be made in due time. As he was entirely at the mercy of his captors, they must look for hope only from that source. If reward was their motive, he was worth more living than dead. This was the only consolation deduced. The letter concluded by advising them to meet any overture in strict confidence. As only money would be acceptable in such a case, the friend pledged all his means in behalf of Don Ramon should it be needed.

These were anxious days and weary nights for this innocent family. The father, no doubt, would welcome death itself in preference to the rack on which he was kept by his captors. Time is not considered valuable in warm climates, and two weary days were allowed to pass before any conversation was renewed with Don Ramon.

Then once more the chief had the fetters

removed from his victim's ankles, with the customary guard within call. He explained that many of the men were away, and it would be several days yet before he could know if the outlook for his release was favorable. From what he had been able to learn so far, at least fifty thousand dollars would be necessary to satisfy the band, which numbered twenty, five of whom were spies. They were poor men, he further explained, many of them had families, and if they accepted money in a case like this, self-banishment was the only safe course, as the political society to which they belonged would place a price on their heads if they were detected.

"The sum mentioned is a large one," commented Don Ramon, "but it is nothing to the mental anguish that I suffer daily. If I had time and freedom, the money might be raised. But as it is, it is doubtful if I could command one fifth of it."

"You have a son," said the chief, "a young man of twenty. Could he not as well as yourself raise this amount? A letter could be placed in his hands stating that a political society had sentenced you to death, and that your life was only spared from day to day by the sufferance of your captors. Ask him to raise this sum, tell him it would mean freedom and restoration to your family. Could he not do this as well as you?"

"If time were given him, possibly. Can I send him such a letter?" pleaded Don Ramon, brightening with the hope of this new opportunity.

"It would be impossible at present. The consent of all interested must first be gained. Our responsibility then becomes greater than yours. No false step must be taken. To-morrow is the soonest that we can get a hearing with all. There must be no dissenters to the plan or it fails, and then — well, the execution has been delayed long enough."

Thus the days wore on.

The absence of the band, except for the few who guarded the prisoner, was policy on their part. They were receiving the news from the river villages daily, where the friends of Don Ramon discussed his absence in whispers. Their system of espionage was as careful as their methods were cruel and heartless. They even got reports from the ranch that not a member of the family had ventured away since its master's capture. The local authorities were inactive. The bandits would play their cards for a high ransom.

Early one morning after a troubled night's rest, Don Ramon was awakened by the arrival

of the robbers, several of whom were bois-
terously drunk. It was only with curses and
drawn arms that the chief prevented these men
from committing outrages on their helpless
captive.

After coffee was served, the chief unfolded
his plot to them, with Don Ramon as a listener
to the proceedings. Addressing them, he said
that the prisoner's offense was not one against
them or theirs; that at best they were but the
hirelings of others; that they were poorly paid,
and that it had become sickening to him to
do the bloody work for others. Don Ramon
Mora had gold at his command, enough to
give each more in a day than they could hope
to receive for years of this inhuman servitude.
He could possibly pay to each two thousand
dollars for his freedom, guaranteeing them his
gratitude, and pledging to refrain from any
prosecution. Would they accept this offer or
refuse it? As many as were in favor of grant-
ing his life would deposit in his hat a leaf from
the mesquite; those opposed, a leaf from the
wild cane which surrounded their camp.

The vote asked for was watched by the
prisoner as only a man could watch whose
life hung in the balance. There were eight
cane leaves to seven of the mesquite. The
chief flew into a rage, cursed his followers for

murderers for refusing to let the life blood run in this man, who had never done one of them an injury. He called them cowards for attacking the helpless, even accusing them of lack of respect for their chief's wishes. The majority hung their heads like whipped curs. When he had finished his harangue, one of their number held up his hand to beg the privilege of speaking.

"Yes, defend your dastardly act if you can," said the chief.

"Capitan," said the man, making obeisance and tapping his breast, "there is an oath recorded here, in memory of a father who was hanged by the French for no other crime save that he was a patriot to the land of his birth. And you ask me to violate my vow! To the wind with your sympathy! To the gallows with our enemies!" There was a chorus of "bravos" and shouts of "Vivi el Mejico," as the majority congratulated the speaker.

When the chief led the prisoner back to his blanket, he spoke hopefully to Don Ramon, explaining that it was the mescal the men had drunk which made them so unreasonable and defiant. Promising to reason with them when they were more sober, he left Don Ramon with his solitary guard. The chief then returned to the band, where he received the congratulations of his partners in crime on his mock sympathy. It was agreed that the majority should be won over at the next council, which they would hold that evening.

The chief returned to his prisoner during the day, and expressed a hope that by evening, when his followers would be perfectly sober, they would listen to reason. He doubted, however, if the sum first named would satisfy them, and insisted that he be authorized to offer more. To this latter proposition Don Ramon made answer, "I am helpless to promise you anything, but if you will only place me in correspondence with my son, all I possess, everything that can be hypothecated shall go to satisfy your demands. Only let it be soon, for this suspense is killing me."

An hour before dark the band was once more summoned together, with Don Ramon in their midst. The chief asked the majority if they had any compromise to offer to his proposition of the morning, and received a negative answer. "Then," said he, "remember that a trusting wife and eight children, the eldest a lad of twenty, the youngest a toddling tot of a girl, claim a husband and a father's love at the hands of the prisoner here. Are you such base ingrates that you can show no mercy, not even to the innocent?"

The majority were abashed, and one by one fell back in the distance. Finally a middle-aged man came forward and said, "Give us five thousand dollars in gold apiece, the money to be in hand, and the prisoner may have his liberty, all other conditions made in the morning to be binding."

"Your answer to that, Don Ramon?" asked the chief.

"I have promised my all. I ask nothing but life. I may have friends who will assist. Give me an opportunity to see what can be done."

"You shall have it," replied the chief, "and on its success depends your liberty or the consequences."

Going amongst the band, he ordered them to meet again in three days at one of their rendezvous near Agua Dulce; to go by twos, visit the river towns on the way, to pick up all items of interest, and particularly to watch for any movement of the authorities.

Retaining two of his companions to act as guards, the others saddled their horses and dispersed by various routes. The chief waited until the moon was well up, then abandoned their camp of the last ten days and set out towards Agua Dulce. To show his friendship for his victim, he removed all irons, but did not give freedom to Don Ramon's horse, which was led, as before.

It was after midnight when they recrossed the river to the American side, using a ford known to but a few smugglers. When day broke they were well inland and secure in the chaparral. Another night's travel, and they were encamped in the place agreed upon. Reports which the members of the band brought to the chief showed that the authorities had made no movement as yet, so evidently this outrage had never been properly reported.

Don Ramon was now furnished paper and pencil, and he addressed a letter to his son and family. The contents can easily be imagined. It concluded with an appeal to secrecy, and an order to observe in confidence and honor any compact made, as his life and liberty depended on it. When this missive had passed the scrutiny of the bandits, it was dispatched by one of their number to Señora Mora. It was just two weeks since Don Ramon's disappearance, a fortnight of untold anguish and uncertainty to his family.

The messenger reached Agua Dulce an hour before midnight, and seeing a light in the house, warned the inmates of his presence by the usual "Ave Maria," a friendly salutation invoking the blessings of the saints on all within hearing. Supposing that some friend had a word for them, the son went outside, meeting the messenger.

"Are you the son of Don Ramon Mora?" asked the bandit.

"I am," replied the young man; "won't you dismount?"

"No. I bear a letter to you from your father. One moment, señor! I have within call half a dozen men. Give no alarm. Read his instructions to you. I shall expect an answer in half an hour. The letter, señor."

The son hastened into the house to read his father's communication. The bandit kept a strict watch over the premises to see that no demonstration was made against him. When the half hour was nearly up, the son came forward and tendered the answer. Passing the compliments of the moment, the man rode away as airily as though the question were of hearts instead of life. The reply was first read by Don Ramon, then turned over to the chief. It would require a second letter, which was to be called for in four days. Things were now nearing the danger point. They must be doubly vigilant; so all but the chief and two guards scattered out and watched every movement. Two or three towns on the river were to have special care. Friends of the family lived in these towns. They must be watched. The officers of the law were the most to be feared. Every bit of conversation overheard was carefully noted, with its effects and bearing.

At the appointed time, another messenger was sent to the ranch, but only a part of the band returned to know the result. The sum which the son reported at his command was very disappointing. It would not satisfy the leaders, and there would be nothing for the others. It was out of the question to consider it. The chief cursed himself for letting his sympathy get the better of him. Why had he not listened to the majority and been true to an accepted duty? He called himself a woman for having acted as he had — a man unfit to be trusted.

Don Ramon heard these self-reproaches of the chief with a heavy heart, and when opportunity occurred, he pleaded for one more chance. He had many friends. There had not been time enough to see them all. His lands and cattle had not been hypothecated. Give him one more chance. Have mercy.

" I was a fool," said the chief, " to listen to a condemned man's hopes, but having gone so far I might as well be hung for a sheep as a lamb." Turning to Don Ramon, he said, "Write your son that if twice the sum named in his letter is not forthcoming within a week, it will be too late."

The chief now became very surly, often declaring that the case was hopeless; that the money could never be raised. He taunted his captive with the fact that he had always considered himself above his neighbors, and that now he could not command means enough to purchase the silence and friendship of a score of beggars! His former kindness changed to cruelty at every opportunity; and he took delight in hurling his venom on his helpless victim.

Dispatching the letter, he ordered the band to scatter as before, appointing a meeting place a number of days hence. After the return of the messenger, he broke camp in the middle of the night, not forgetting to add other indignities to the heavy irons already on his victim. During the ensuing time they traveled the greater portion of each night. To the prisoner's questions as to where they were he received only insulting replies. His inquiries served only to suggest other cruelties. One night they set out unusually early, the chief saying that they would recross the river before morning, so that if the ransom was not satisfactory, the execution might take place at once. On this night the victim was blindfolded. After many hours of riding — it was nearly morning when they halted — the bandage was removed from his eyes, and he was asked if he knew the place.

"Yes, it is Agua Dulce."

The moon shone over its white stone buildings, quietly sleeping in the still hours of the night, as over the white, silent slabs of a country churchyard. Not a sound could be heard from any living thing. They dismounted and gagged their prisoner. Tying their horses at a respectable distance, they led their victim toward his home. Don Ramon was a small man, and could offer no resistance to his captors. They cautioned him that the slightest resistance would mean death, while compliance to their wishes carried a hope of life.

Cautiously and with a stealthy step, they advanced like the thieves they were, their victim in the iron grasp of two strong guards, while a rope with a running noose around his neck, in the hands of the chief, made their gag doubly effective. A garden wall ran within a few feet of the rear of the house, and behind it they crouched. The only sound was the labored breathing of their prisoner. Hark! the cry of a child is heard within the house.

Oh, God! it is his child, his baby girl. Listen! The ear of the mother has heard it, and her soothing voice has reached his anxious ear. His wife — the mother of his children — is now bending over their baby's crib. The muscles of Don Ramon's arms turn to iron. His eyes flash defiance at the grinning fiends who exult at his misery. The running noose tightens on his neck, and he gasps for breath. As they lead him back to his horse, his brain seems on fire; he questions his own sanity, even the mercy of Heaven.

When the sun arose that morning, they were far away in one of the impenetrable thickets in which the country abounded. Since his capture Don Ramon had suffered, but never as now. Death would have been preferable, not that life had no claims upon him, but that he no longer had hopes of liberty. The uncertainty was unbearable. The bandits exercised caution enough to keep all means of self-destruction out of his reach. Hardened as they were, they noticed that their last racking of the prisoner had benumbed even hope.

Sleep alone was kind to him, though he usually awoke to find his dreams a mockery. That night the answer to the second demand would arrive. A number of the band came in during the day and brought the rumor that

the governor of the State had been notified
of their high-handed actions. It was thought
that a company of Texas Rangers would be
ordered to the Rio Grande. This meant action, and soon. When the reply came from
the son of Don Ramon, he was notified to have
the money ready at a certain abandoned ranchita, though the amount, now increased, was
not as large as was expected. It required two
days longer for the delivery, which was to be
made at midnight, and to be accompanied by
not over two messengers.

At this juncture, a squad of ten Texas Rangers disembarked at the nearest point on the
railroad to this river village. The emergency
appeal, which had finally reached the governor's ear, was acted upon promptly, and
though the men seemed very few in number,
they were tried, experienced, fearless Rangers,
from the crack company of the State. There
was no waste of time after leaving the train.
The little command set out apparently for the
river home of Don Ramon, distant nearly a
hundred miles. After darkness had set in, the
captain of the squad cut his already small
command in two, sending a lieutenant with
four men to proceed by way of Agua Dulce
ranch, the remainder continuing on to the
river. The captain refused them even pack

horse or blanket, allowing them only their arms. He instructed them to call themselves cowboys, and in case they met any Mexicans, to make inquiries for a well-known American ranch which was located in the chaparral. With a few simple instructions from his superior, the lieutenant and squad rode away into the darkness of a June night.

It was in reality the dark hour before dawn when they reached Agua Dulce. As secretly as possible the lieutenant aroused Don Ramon's wife and sought an interview with her. Speaking Spanish fluently, he explained his errand and her duty to put him in possession of all the facts in the case. Bewildered, as any gentlewoman would be under the circumstances, she reluctantly told the main facts. This officer treated Señora Mora with every courtesy, and was eventually rewarded when she requested him and his men to remain her guests until her son should return, which would be before noon. She explained that he would bring a large sum of money with him, which was to be the ransom price of her husband, and which was to be paid over at midnight within twenty miles of Agua Dulce. This information was food and raiment to the Ranger.

The señora of Agua Dulce sent a servant

to secrete the Ranger's horses in a near-by pasture, and with saddles hidden inside the house, before the people of the ranch or the sun arose, five Rangers were sleeping under the roof of the *Casa primero.*

It was late in the day when the lieutenant awoke to find Don Ramon, Jr., ready to welcome and join in furnishing any details unknown to his mother. The commercial instincts of the young man sided with the Rangers, but the mother — thank God! — knew no such impulses and thought of nothing save the return of her husband, the father of her brood. The officer considered only duty — sentiment being an unknown quantity to him. He assured his hostess that if she would confide in them, her husband would be returned to her with all dispatch. Concealing such things as he considered advisable from both mother and son, he outlined his plans. At the appointed time and place the money should be paid over and the compact adhered to to the letter. He reserved to himself and company, however, to furnish any red light necessary.

An hour after dark, a messenger, Don Ramon, Jr., and five Rangers set out to fulfill all contracts pending and understood. The abandoned ranchita in the *monte* — the meeting point — had been at one time a stone house of some pretensions, where had formerly lived its builder, a wealthy, eccentric recluse. It had in previous years, however, been burned, so that now only crumbling walls remained, a gloomy, isolated, though picturesque ruin, standing in an opening several acres in extent, while trails, once in use, led to and from it.

When the party arrived within two miles of the meeting point, an hour in advance of the appointed time, a halt was called. Under the direction of the lieutenant, the son and his companion were to proceed by an old trail, forsaking the regular pathway leading from Agua Dulce to the old ranch. The Ranger squad tied their horses and followed a respectful distance behind, near enough, however, to hear in case any guards might halt them. They were carefully cautioned not even to let Don Ramon, if he were present, know that rescue from another quarter was at hand. When the two sighted the ruin they noticed a dim light within the walls. Then, without a single challenge, they dashed up to the old house, amid a clatter of hoofs, and shouts of welcome from the bandits.

The messengers were unarmed, and once inside the house were made prisoners, ironed, and ordered into a corner, where crouched

Don Ramon Mora, now enfeebled by mental racking and physical abuse. The meeting of father and son will be spared the reader, yet in the young man's heart was a hope that he dared not communicate.

The night was warm. A fire flickered in the old fireplace, and around its circle gathered nine bandits to count and gloat over the blood money of their victim, as a miser might over his bags of gold. The bottle passed freely round the circle, and with toast and taunt and jeer the counting of the money was progressing. Suddenly, and with as little warning as if they had dropped down from among the stars, five Texas Rangers sprang through windows and doors, and without a word a flood of fire frothed from the mouths of ten six-shooters, hurling death into the circle about the fire. There was no cessation of the rain of lead until every gun was emptied, when the men sprang back, each to his window or door, where a carbine, carefully left, awaited his hand to complete the work of death. In the few moments that elapsed, the smoke arose and the fire burned afresh, revealing the accuracy of their aim. As they reëntered to review their work, two of the bandits were found alive and untouched, having thrown themselves in a corner amid the confusion of smoke in the onslaught. Thus they were spared the fate of the others, though the ghastly sight of seven of their number, translated from life into death, met their terrorized gaze. Human blood streamed across the once peaceful hearth, while brains bespattered life-sized figures in bas-relief of the Virgin Mary and Christ Child which adorned the broad columns on either side of the ample fireplace. In the throes of death, one bandit had floundered about until his hand rested in the fire, producing a sickening smell from the burning flesh.

As Don Ramon was released, he stood for a few moments half dazed, looking in bewilderment at the awful spectacle before him. Then as the truth gradually dawned upon him, — that this sacrifice of blood meant liberty to himself, — he fell upon his knees among the still warm bodies of his tormentors, his face raised to the Virgin in exultation of joy and thanksgiving.

XI

THE PASSING OF PEG–LEG

IN the early part of September, '91, the
eastern overland express on the Denver
and Rio Grande was held up and robbed
at Texas Creek. The place is little more
than a watering-station on that line, but it was
an inviting place for hold-ups.

Surrounded by the fastnesses of the front
range of the Rockies, Peg-Leg Eldridge and
his band selected this lonely station as best
fitted for the transaction in hand. To the
southwest lay the Sangre de Cristo range, in
which the band had rendezvoused and planned
this robbery. Farther to the southwest arose
the snow-capped peaks of the Continental Divide, in whose silent solitude an army might
have taken refuge and hidden.

It was an inviting country to the robber.
These mountains offered retreats that had
never known the tread of human footsteps.
Emboldened by the thought that pursuit
would be almost a matter of impossibility, they
laid their plans and executed them without a
single hitch.

About ten o'clock at night, as the train slowed up as usual to take water, the engineer and fireman were covered by two of the robbers. The other two — there were only four — cut the express car from the train, and the engineer and fireman were ordered to decamp. The robbers ran the engine and express car out nearly two miles, where, by the aid of dynamite, they made short work of a through safe that the messenger could not open. The express company concealed the amount of money lost to the robbers, but smelters, who were aware of certain retorts in transit by this train, were not so silent. These smelter products were in gold retorts of such a size that they could be made away with as easily as though they had reached the mint and been coined.

There was scarcely any excitement among the passengers, so quickly was it over. While the robbery was in progress the wires from this station were flashing the news to headquarters. At a division of the railroad one hundred and fifty-six miles distant from the scene of the robbery, lived United States Marshal Bob Banks, whose success in pursuing criminals was not bounded by the State in which he lived. His reputation was in a large measure due to the successful use of bloodhounds. This officer's calling compelled him to be both plainsman and mountaineer. He had the well-deserved reputation of being as unrelenting in the pursuit of criminals as death is in marking its victims.

Within half an hour after the robbery was reported at headquarters, an engine had coupled to a caboose at the division where the marshal lived. He was equally hasty. To gather his arms and get his dogs aboard the caboose required but a few moments' time.

Everything ready, they pulled out with a clear track to their destination. Heavy traffic in coal had almost ruined the road-bed, but engine and caboose flew over it regardless of its condition. Halfway to their destination the marshal was joined by several officials, both railway and express. From there the train turned westward, up the valley of the Arkansas. Here was a track and an occasion that gave the most daring engineer license to throw the throttle wide open.

The climax of this night's run was through the Grand Cañon of the Arkansas. Into this gash in the earth's surface plunged the engineer, as though it were an easy stretch of down-grade prairie. As the engine rounded turns, the headlight threw its rays up serried columns of granite half a mile high, — columns that rear their height in grotesque form and Gothic arch, polished by the waters of ages.

As the officials agreed, after a full discussion with the marshal of every phase and possibility of capture, the hope of this night's work and the punishment of the robbers rested almost entirely on three dogs lying on the floor, and, as the rocking of the car disturbed them, growling in their dreams. In their helplessness to cope with this outrage, they turned to these dumb animals as a welcome ally. Under the guidance of their master they were an aid whose value he well understood. Their sense of smell was more reliable than the sense of seeing in man. You can believe the dog when you doubt your own eyes. His opinion is unquestionably correct.

As the train left the cañon it was but a short run to the scene of the depredation. During the night the few people who resided at this station were kept busy getting together saddle-horses for the officer's posse. This was not easily done, as there were few horses at the station, while the horses of near-by ranches were turned loose in the open range for the night. However, upon the arrival of the train, Banks and the express people found mounts awaiting them to carry them to the place of the hold-up.

After the robbers had finished their work during the fore part of the night, the train crew went out and brought back to the station the engine and express car. The engine was unhurt, but the express car was badly shattered, and the through safe was ruined by the successive charges of dynamite that were used to force it to yield up its treasure. The local safe was unharmed, the messenger having opened it in order to save it from the fate of its larger and stronger brother. The train proceeded on its way, with the loss of a few hours' time and the treasure of its express.

Day was breaking in the east as the posse reached the scene. The marshal lost no time circling about until the trail leaving was taken up. Even the temporary camp of the robbers was found in close proximity to the chosen spot. The experienced eye of this officer soon determined the number of men, though they led several horses. It was a cool, daring act of Peg-Leg and three men. Afterward, when his past history was learned, his leadership in this raid was established.

Peg-Leg Eldridge was a product of that unfortunate era succeeding the civil war. During that strife the herds of the southwest were neglected to such an extent that thousands of cattle grew to maturity without earmark or brand to identify their owner. A good mount of horses, a rope and a running-iron in the hands of a capable man, were better than capital. The good old days when an active young man could brand annually fifteen calves—all better than yearlings— to every cow he owned, are looked back to to this day, from cattle king to the humblest of the craft, in pleasant reminiscence, though they will come no more. Eldridge was of that time, and when conditions changed, he failed to change with them. This was the reason that, under the changed condition of affairs, he frequently got his brand on some other man's calf. This resulted in his losing a leg from a gunshot at the hands of a man he had thus outraged. Worse, it branded him for all time as a cattle thief, with every man's hand against him. Thus the steps that led up to this September night were easy, natural, and gradual. This child of circumstances, a born plainsman like the Indian, read in plain, forest, and mountain, things which were not visible to other eyes. The stars were his compass by night, the heat waves of the plain warned him of the tempting mirage, while the cloud on the mountain's peak or the wind in the pines which sheltered him alike spoke to him and he understood.

The robbers' trail was followed but a few miles, when their course was well established. They were heading into the Sangre de Cristo Mountains. Several hours were lost here by the pursuing party, as they were compelled to await the arrival of a number of pack horses; so when the trail was taken up in earnest they were at least twelve hours behind the robbers.

In the ascent of the foot-hills the dogs led the posse, six in number, a merry chase. As they gradually rose to higher altitudes the trail of the robbers was more compact and easy to follow, except for the roughness of the mountain slope. Frequently the trail was but a single narrow path. Old game trails, where the elk and deer, drifting in the advance of winter, crossed the range, had been followed by the robbers. These game trails were certain to lead to the passes in the range. Thus, by the instinct given to the deer and elk against the winter's storm, the humblest of His creatures had blazed for these train robbers an unerring pathway to the mountain's pass.

Along these paths the trail was so distinct that the dogs were an unnecessary adjunct to the pursuing party. These hounds, one of which was a veteran in the service, while the other two, being younger, were without that practice which perfects, showed an exuberance of energy and ambition in following the trail. The ancestry of the dogs was Russian. Hounds of this breed never give mouth, thus warning the hunted of their approach. Man-hunting is exciting sport. The possibility, though the trail may look hours old, that any turn of the trail may disclose the fugitives, keeps at the highest tension every nerve of the pursuer.

All day long the marshal and posse climbed higher and higher on the rugged mountain-side. Night came on as they reached the narrow plateau that formed the crest of the mountain, on which they found several small parks. Here they made the first halt since the start in the morning. The necessity of resting their saddle stock was very apparent to Banks, though he would gladly have pushed on. The only halt he could expect of the robbers was to save their own horses, and he must do the same. Forcing a tired horse an extra hour has left many an amateur rider afoot. He real-ized this. Knowing the necessity of being well mounted, the robbers had no doubt splendid horses. This was a reasonable supposition.

Near midnight the marshal and posse set out once moré on the trail. He was compelled to take it afoot now, depending on his favorite dog, which was under leash, the posse following with the mounts. The dogs led them several miles southward on this mountain crest. Here was where the dogs were valuable. The robbers had traveled in some places an entire mile over lava beds, not leaving as much as a trace which the eye could detect. Having the advantage of daylight, the robbers selected a rocky cliff, over which they began the descent of the western slope of this range. The ingenuity displayed by them to throw pursuit from their trail marked Peg-Leg as an artist in his calling. But with the aid of dogs and the dampness of night, their trail was as easily followed as though it had been made in snow.

This declivity was rough, and in places every one was compelled to dismount. Progress was extremely slow, and when the rising sun tipped the peaks of the Continental Range, before them lay the beautiful landscape where the Rio Grande in a hundred mountain streams has her fountain-head. With only a few hours' rest for men and animals during the day, night fell upon them before they had reached the mesa at the foot-hills on the western slope. An hour before nightfall they came upon the first camp or halt of the robbers. They had evidently spent but a short time here, there being no indication that they had slept. Criminals are inured to all kinds of hardship. They have been known to go for days without sleep, while smugglers, well mounted, have put a hundred miles of country behind them in a single night.

The marshal and party pushed forward during the night, the country being more favorable. When morning came they had covered many a mile, and it was believed they had made time, as the trail seemed fresher. There were several ranches along the main stream in the valley, which the robbers had avoided with well-studied caution, showing that they had passed through in the daytime. There are several lines of railroad running through this valley section. These they crossed at points between stations, where observation would be almost impossible either by day or night. Inquiries at ranches failed on account of the lack of all accurate means of description. The posse was maintaining a due southwest course that was carrying them into the fastnesses of the main range of the western continent. Another full day of almost constant advance, and the trail had entered the undulating hills forming the approach of this second range of mountains. Physical exertion was beginning to tell on the animals, and they were compelled to make frequent halts in the ascent of this range.

The fatigue was showing in the two younger

dogs. Their feet had been cut in several places in crossing the first range of mountains. During the past nights in the valley, though their master was keeping a sharp lookout, they encountered several places where sand-burrs were plentiful. These burrs in the tender inner part of a dog's foot, if not removed at once, soon lame it. Many times had the poor creatures lain down, licking their paws in anguish. On examination during the previous night, their feet were found to be webbed with this burr. Now, on climbing this second mountain, they began to show the lameness which their master so much feared, until it was almost impossible to make them take any interest in the trail. The old dog, however, seemed nothing the worse for his work.

On reaching the first small park near the summit of this range, the pursuers were so exhausted that they lay down and took their first sleep, having been over three days and a half on the trail. The marshal himself slept several hours, but he was the last to go to sleep and the first to awake. Before going to sleep, and on arising, he was particular to bathe the dogs' feet. The nearest approach to a liniment that he possessed was a lubricating tube for guns, which he fortunately had with him. This afforded relief.

It was daybreak when the pursuers took up the trail. The plateau on the crest of this range was in places several miles wide, having a luxuriant growth of grass upon it. The course of the robbers continued to the southwest. The pursuers kept this plateau for several miles, and before descending the western slope of the range an abandoned camp was found, where the pursued had evidently made their first bunks. Indications of where horses had been picketed for hours, and where both men and horses had slept were evident. The trail where it left this deserted camp was in no wise encouraging to the marshal, as it looked at least thirty-six hours old. As the pursuers began the descent, they could see below them where the San Juan River meanders to the west until her waters, mingling with others, find their outlet into the Pacific. It was a trial of incessant toil down the mountain slope, wearisome alike to man and beast. Near the foot-hill of this mountain they were rewarded by finding a horse which the robbers had abandoned on account of an accident. He was an extremely fine horse, but so lame in the shoulders, apparently owing to a fall, that it was impossible to move him. The trail of the robbers kept in the foot-hills, finally doubling back an almost due east course. Now and then ranches were visible out on the mesa, but in all instances they were carefully avoided by the pursued.

Spending a night in these hills, the posse prepared to make an early start. Here, however, they met their first serious trouble. Both of the younger dogs had feet so badly swollen that it was impossible to make them take any interest in the trail. After doing everything possible for them, their owner sent them to a ranch which was in sight several miles below in the valley. Several hours were lost to the party by this incident, though they were in no wise deterred in following the trail, still having the veteran dog. Late that afternoon they met a *pastor*, who gave them a description of the robbers.

" Yesterday morning," said the shepherd, in broken Spanish, " shortly after daybreak, four men rode into my camp and asked for breakfast. I gave them coffee, but as I had no meat in my quarters, they tried to buy a lamb, which I have no right to sell. After drinking the coffee they tendered me money, which I refused. On leaving, one of their number rode into my flock and killed a kid. Taking it with him, he rode away with the others."

A good description of the robbers was secured from this simple shepherd, — a full description of men, horses, colors, and condition of pack. The next day nothing of importance developed, and the posse hugged the shelter of the hills skirting the mountain range, crossing into New Mexico. It was late that night when they went into camp on the trail. They had pushed forward with every energy, hoping to lessen the intervening distance between them and the robbers. The following morning on awakening, to the surprise and mortification of everybody, the old dog was unable to stand upon his feet. While this was felt to be a serious drawback, it did not necessarily check the chase.

In bringing to bay over thirty criminals, one of whom had paid the penalty of his crime on the gallows, master and dog had heretofore been an invincible team. Old age and physical weakness had now overtaken the dog in an important chase, and the sympathy he deserved was not withheld, nor was he deserted. Tenderly as a mother would lift a sick child, Banks gathered him in his arms and lifted him to one of the posse on his horse. To the members of the posse it was a touching scene: they remembered him but a few months before pursuing a flying criminal, when the latter — seeing that escape was impossible and turning to draw his own weapon upon the

officer, whose six-shooter had been emptied
at the fugitive, but who with drawn knife was
ready to close with him in the death struggle
— immediately threw down his weapon and
pleaded for his life.

Yet this same officer could not keep back
the tears that came into his eyes as he lifted
this dumb comrade of other victories to a
horse. With an earnest oath he brushed the
incident away by assuring his posse that unless
the earth opened and swallowed up the robbers they could not escape. A few hours after
taking up the trail, a ranch was sighted and
the dog was left, the instructions of the Good
Samaritan being repeated. At this ranch they
succeeded in buying two fresh horses, which
proved a valuable addition to their mounts.

Now it became a hunt of man by man. To
an experienced trailer like the marshal there
was little difficulty in keeping the trail. That
the robbers kept to the outlying country was
an advantage. Yet the latter traveled both
night and day, while pursuit must of necessity
be by day only. With the fresh horses secured,
they covered a stretch of country hardly cred-
ible.

During the day they found a place where
the robbers had camped for at least a full day.
A trail made by two horses had left this

camp, and returned. The marshal had followed it to a rather pretentious Mexican rancho, where there was a small store kept. Here a second description of the two men was secured, though neither one was Peg-Leg. He was so indelibly marked that he was crafty enough to keep out of sight of so public a place as a store. These two had tried unsuccessfully to buy horses at this rancho.

The next morning the representative of the express company left the posse to report progress. He was enabled to give such an exact description of the robbers that the company, through their detective system, were not long in locating the leader. The marshal and posse pushed on with the same unremitting energy. The trail was now almost due east. The population of the country was principally Mexican, and even Mexicans the robbers avoided as much as possible. They had, however, bought horses at several ranches, and were always liberal in the use of money, but very exacting in regard to the quality of horseflesh they purchased; the best was none too good for them. They passed north of old Santa Fé town, and entering a station on the line of railway by that name late at night, they were liberal patrons of the gaming tables that the town tolerated. The next morning they had disappeared.

At no time did the pursuers come within two days of them. This was owing to the fact that they traveled by night as well as day. At the last-mentioned point messages were exchanged with the express company with little loss of time. Banks had asked that certain points on the railway be watched in the hope of capture while crossing the country, but the effort was barren of results. In following the trail the marshal had recrossed the continuation of the first range of mountains which they had crossed to the west ten days before, or the morning after the robbery, three hundred miles southward. There was nothing difficult in the passage of this range of mountains, and now before them stretched the endless prairie to the eastward. Here Banks seriously felt the loss of his dogs. This was a country that they could be used in to good advantage. It would then be a question of endurance of men and horses. As it was, he could work only by day. Two lines of railway were yet to be crossed if the band held its course. The same tactics were resorted to as formerly, yet this vigilance and precaution availed nothing, as Peg-Leg crossed them carefully between two of the watched places. Owing to his occupation, he knew the country better by night than day.

Banks was met by the officials of the express

company on one of these lines of railroad. The exhaustive amount of information that they had been able to collect regarding this interesting man with the wooden leg was astonishing. From out of the abundance of the data there were a few items that were of interest to the officer. Several of Eldridge's haunts when not actively engaged in his profession were located. In one of these haunts was a woman, and toward this one he was heading, though it was many a weary mile distant.

At the marshal's request the express people had brought bloodhounds with them. The dogs proved worthless, and the second day were abandoned. When the trail crossed the Gulf Railway the robbers were three days ahead. The posse had now been fourteen days on the trail. Banks followed them one day farther, himself alone, leaving his tired companions at a station near the line of the Panhandle of Texas. This extra day's ride was to satisfy himself that the robbers were making for one of their haunts. They kept, as he expected, down between the two Canadians.

After following the trail until he was thoroughly satisfied of their destination, the marshal retraced his steps and rejoined his posse.

The first train carried him and the posse back to the headquarters of the express company.

Two weeks later, at a country store in the Chickasaw Nation, there was a horse race of considerable importance. The country side were gathered to witness it. The owners of the horses had made large wagers on the race. Outsiders wagered money and livestock to a large amount. There were a number of strangers present, which was nothing unusual. As the race was being run and every eye was centred on the outcome, a stranger present put a six-shooter to a very interested spectator's ear, and informed him that he was a prisoner. Another stranger did the same thing to another spectator. They also snapped handcuffs on both of them. One of these spectators had a peg-leg. They were escorted to a waiting rig, and when they alighted from it were on the line of a railroad forty miles distant. One of these strangers was a United States marshal, who for the past month had been very anxious to meet these same gentlemen.

Once safe from the rescue of friends of these robbers, the marshal regaled his guest with the story of the chase, which had now terminated. He was even able to give Eldridge a good part of his history. But when he attempted to draw him out as to the whereabouts of the other two, Peg was sullenly ignorant of anything. They were never captured, having separated before reaching the haunt of Mr. Eldridge. Eldridge was tried in a Federal court in Colorado and convicted of train robbery. He went over the road for a term of years far beyond the lease of his natural life. He, with the companion captured at the same time, was taken by an officer of the court to Detroit for confinement. When within an hour's ride of the prison — his living grave — he raised his ironed hands, and twisting from a blue flannel shirt which he wore a large pearl button, said to the officer in charge: —

"Will you please take this button back and give it, with my compliments, to that human bloodhound, and say to him that I'm sorry that I did n't anticipate meeting him? If I had, it would have saved you this trip with me. He might have got me, but I would n't have needed a trial when he did."

XII

IN THE HANDS OF HIS FRIENDS

THERE was a painting at the World's Fair at Chicago named "The Reply," in which the lines of two contending armies were distinctly outlined. One of these armies had demanded the surrender of the other. The reply was being written by a little fellow, surrounded by grim veterans of war. He was not even a soldier. But in this little fellow's countenance shone a supreme contempt for the enemy's demand. His patriotism beamed out as plainly as did that of the officer dictating to him. Physically he was debarred from being a soldier ; still there was a place where he could be useful.

So with Little Jack Martin. He was a cripple and could not ride, but he could cook. If the way to rule men is through the stomach, Jack was a general who never knew defeat. The "J + H" camp, where he presided over the kitchen, was noted for good living. Jack's domestic tastes followed him wherever he went, so that he surrounded himself at this camp with chickens, and a few cows for milk.

During the spring months, when the boys were away on the various round-ups, he planted and raised a fine garden. Men returning from a hard month's work would brace themselves against fried chicken, eggs, milk, and fresh vegetables. After drinking alkali water for a month and living out of tin cans, who wouldn't love Jack? In addition to his garden, he always raised a fine patch of watermelons. This camp was an oasis in the desert. Every man was Jack's friend, and an enemy was an unknown personage. The peculiarity about him, aside from his deformity, was his ability to act so much better than he could talk. In fact he could barely express his simplest wants in words.

Cripples are usually cross, irritable, and unpleasant companions. Jack was the reverse. His best qualities shone their brightest when there were a dozen men around to cook for. When they ate heartily he felt he was useful. If a boy was sick, Jack could make a broth, or fix a cup of beef tea like a mother or sister. When he went out with the wagon during beef-shipping season, a pot of coffee simmered over the fire all night for the boys on night herd. Men going or returning on guard liked to eat. The bread and meat left over from the meals of the day were always left convenient for the boys. It was the many little things that he thought of which made him such a general favorite with every one.

Little Jack was middle-aged when the proclamation of the President opening the original Oklahoma was issued. This land was to be thrown open in April. It was not a cow-country then, though it had been once. There was a warning in this that the Strip would be next. The dominion of the cowman was giving way to the homesteader. One day Jack found opportunity to take Miller, our foreman, into his confidence. They had been together five or six years. Jack had coveted a spot in the section which was to be thrown open, and he asked the foreman to help him get it. He had been all over the country when it was part of the range, and had picked out a spot on Big Turkey Creek, ten miles south of the Strip line. It gradually passed from one to another of us what Jack wanted. At first we felt blue about it, but Miller, who could see farther than the rest of us, dispelled the gloom by announcing at dinner, "Jack is going to take a claim if this outfit has a horse in it and a man to ride him. It is only a question of a year or two at the farthest until the rest of us will be guiding a white mule between two corn rows, and glad of the chance. If Jack goes now, he will have just that many years the start of the rest of us."

We nerved ourselves and tried to appear jolly after this talk of the foreman. We entered into quite a discussion as to which horse would be the best to make the ride with. The ranch had several specially good saddle animals. In chasing gray wolves in the winter those qualities of endurance which long races developed in hunting these enemies of cattle, pointed out a certain coyote-colored horse, whose color marks and "Dead Tree" brand indicated that he was of Spanish extraction. Intelligently ridden with a light rider he was First Choice on which to make this run. That was finally agreed to by all. There was no trouble selecting the rider for this horse with the zebra marks. The lightest weight was Billy Edwards. This qualification gave him the preference over us all.

Jack described the spot he desired to claim by an old branding-pen which had been built there when it had been part of the range. Billy had ironed up many a calf in those same pens himself. "Well, Jack," said Billy, "if this outfit don't put you on the best quarter section around that old corral, you'll know that they have throwed off on you."

It was two weeks before the opening day. The coyote horse was given special care from this time forward. He feasted on corn, while others had to be content with grass. In spite of all the bravado that was being thrown into these preparations, there was noticeable a deep undercurrent of regret. Jack was going from us. Every one wanted him to go, still these dissolving ties moved the simple men to acts of boyish kindness. Each tried to outdo the others, in the matter of a parting present to Jack. He could have robbed us then. It was as bad as a funeral. Once before we felt similarly when one of the boys died at camp. It was like an only sister leaving the family circle.

Miller seemed to enjoy the discomfiture of the rest of us. This creedless old Christian had fine strata in his make-up. He and Jack planned continually for the future. In fact they did n't live in the present like the rest of us. Two days before the opening, we loaded up a wagon with Jack's effects. Every man but the newly installed cook went along. It was too early in the spring for work to commence. We all dubbed Jack a boomer from this time forward. The horse so much depended on was led behind the wagon.

On the border we found a motley crowd of

people. Soldiers had gathered them into camps along the line to prevent "sooners" from entering before the appointed time. We stopped in a camp directly north of the claim our little boomer wanted. One thing was certain, it would take a better horse than ours to win the claim away from us. No sooner could take it. That and other things were what all of us were going along for.

The next day when the word was given that made the land public domain, Billy was in line on the coyote. He held his place to the front with the best of them. After the first few miles, the others followed the valley of Turkey Creek, but he maintained his course like wild fowl, skirting the timber which covered the first range of hills back from the creek. Jack followed with the wagon, while the rest of us rode leisurely, after the first mile or so. When we saw Edwards bear straight ahead from the others, we argued that a sooner only could beat us for the claim. If he tried to out-hold us, it would be six to one, as we noticed the leaders closely when we slacked up. By not following the valley, Billy would cut off two miles. Any man who could ride twelve miles to the coyote's ten with Billy Edwards in the saddle was welcome to the earth. That was the way we felt. We rode together, expecting to make the claim three quarters of an hour behind our man. When near enough to sight it, we could see Billy and another horseman apparently protesting with one another. A loud yell from one of us attracted our man's attention. He mounted his horse and rode out and met us. "Well, fellows, it's the expected that's happened this time," said he. "Yes, there's a sooner on it, and he puts up a fine bluff of having ridden from the line ; but he's a liar by the watch, for there isn't a wet hair on his horse, while the sweat was dripping from the fetlocks of this one."

"If you are satisfied that he is a sooner," said Miller, "he has to go."

"Well, he is a lying sooner," said Edwards.

We reined in our horses and held a short parley. After a brief discussion of the situation, Miller said to us: "You boys go down to him, — don't hurt him or get hurt, but make out that you're going to hang him. Put plenty of reality into it, and I'll come in in time to save him and give him a chance to run for his life."

We all rode down towards him, Miller bearing off towards the right of the old corral, — rode out over the claim noticing the rich soil thrown up by the mole-hills. When we came up to our sooner, all of us dismounted. Edwards confronted him and said, " Do you contest my right to this claim?"

" I certainly do," was the reply.

"Well, you won't do so long," said Edwards. Quick as a flash Mouse prodded the cold steel muzzle of a six-shooter against his ear. As the sooner turned his head and looked into Mouse's stern countenance, one of the boys relieved him of an ugly gun and knife that dangled from his belt. " Get on your horse," said Mouse, emphasizing his demand with an oath, while the muzzle of a forty-five in his ear made the order undebatable. Edwards took the horse by the bits and started for a large black-jack tree which stood near by. Reaching it, Edwards said, " Better use Coon's rope; it's manilla and stronger. Can any of you boys tie a hangman's knot?" he inquired when the rope was handed him.

" Yes, let me," responded several.

" Which limb will be best?" inquired Mouse.

" Take this horse by the bits," said Edwards to one of the boys, "till I look." He coiled the rope sailor fashion, and made an ineffectual attempt to throw it over a large limb which hung out like a yard-arm, but the small branches intervening defeated his throw. While he was coiling the rope to make a second throw, some one said, "Mebby so he'd like to pray."

"What! him pray?" said Edwards. "Any prayer that he might offer could n't get a hearing amongst men, let alone above, where liars are forbidden."

"Try that other limb," said Coon to Edwards; "there's not so much brush in the way; we want to get this job done sometime today." As Edwards made a successful throw, he said, "Bring that horse directly underneath." At this moment Miller dashed up and demanded, "What in hell are you trying to do?"

"This sheep-thief of a sooner contests my right to this claim," snapped Edwards, "and he has played his last cards on this earth. Lead that horse under here."

"Just one moment," said Miller. "I think I know this man — think he worked for me once in New Mexico." The sooner looked at Miller appealingly, his face blanched to whiteness. Miller took the bridle reins out of the hands of the boy who was holding the horse, and whispering something to the sooner said to us, "Are you all ready?"

"Just waiting on you," said Edwards. The sooner gathered up the reins. Miller turned the horse halfway round as though he was going to lead him under the tree, gave him a slap in the flank with his hand, and the sooner, throwing the rowels of his spurs into the horse, shot out from us like a startled deer. We called to him to halt, as half a dozen six-shooters encouraged him to go by opening a fusillade on the fleeing horseman, who only hit the high places while going. Nor did we let up fogging him until we emptied our guns and he entered the timber. There was plenty of zeal in this latter part, as the lead must have zipped and cried near enough to give it reality. Our object was to shoot as near as possible without hitting.

Other horsemen put in an appearance as we were unsaddling and preparing to camp, for we had come to stay a week if necessary. In about an hour Jack joined us, speechless as usual, his face wreathed in smiles. The first step toward a home he could call his own had been taken. We told him about the trouble we had had with the sooner, a story which he seemed to question, until Miller confirmed it. We put up a tent among the black-jacks, as the nights were cool, and were soon at peace with all the world.

At supper that evening Edwards said: "When the old settlers hold their reunions in the next generation, they'll say, 'Thirty years ago Uncle Jack Martin settled over there on Big Turkey,' and point him out to their children as one of the pioneer fathers."

No one found trouble in getting to sleep that night, and the next day arts long forgotten by most of us were revived. Some plowed up the old branding-pen for a garden. Others cut logs for a cabin. Every one did two ordinary days' work. The getting of the logs together was the hardest. We sawed and chopped and hewed for dear life. The first few days Jack and one of the boys planted a fine big garden. On the fourth day we gave up the tent, as the smoke curled upward from our own chimney, in the way that it does in well-told stories. The last night we spent with Jack was one long to be remembered. A bright fire snapped and crackled in the ample fireplace. Every one told stories. Several of the boys could sing "The Lone Star Cow-trail," while "Sam Bass" and "Bonnie Black Bess" were given with a vim.

The next morning we were to leave for camp. One of the boys who would work for us that summer, but whose name was not on the pay-roll until the round-up, stayed with Jack. We all went home feeling fine, and leaving Jack happy as a bird in his new possession. As we were saddling up to leave,

Miller said to Jack, "Now if you're any good, you'll delude some girl to keep house for you 'twixt now and fall. Remember what the Holy Book says about it being hard luck for man to be alone. You notice all your boomer neighbors have wives. That's a hint to you to do likewise."

We were on the point of mounting, when the coyote horse began to act up in great shape. Some one said to Edwards, "Loosen your cinches!" "Oh, it's nothing but the corn he's been eating and a few days' rest," said Miller. "He's just running a little bluff on Billy." As Edwards went to put his foot in the stirrup a second time, the coyote reared like a circus horse. "Now look here, colty," said Billy, speaking to the horse, "my daddy rode with Old John Morgan, the Confederate cavalry raider, and he'd be ashamed of any boy he ever raised that couldn't ride a bad horse like you. You're plum foolish to act this way. Do you think I'll walk and lead you home?" He led him out a few rods from the others and mounted him without any trouble. "He just wants to show Jack how it affects a cow-horse to graze a few days on a boomer's claim,—that's all," said Edwards, when he joined us.

"Now, Jack," said Miller, as a final parting,

" if you want a cow, I'll send one down, or if
you need anything, let us know and we'll come
a-running. It's a bad example you've set us
to go booming this way, but we want to make
a howling success out of you, so we can visit
you next winter. And mind what I told you
about getting married," he called back as he
rode away.

We reached camp by late noon. Miller kept
up his talk about what a fine move Jack had
made ; said that we must get him a stray beef
for his next winter's meat ; kept figuring con-
stantly what else he could do for Jack. "You
come around in a few years and you'll find
him as cosy as a coon, and better off than any
of us," said Miller, when we were talking
about his farming. "I've slept under wet blankets with him, and watched him kindle a fire
in the snow, too often not to know what he's
made of. There's good stuff in that little
rascal."

About the ranch it seemed lonesome without
Jack. It was like coming home from school
when we were kids and finding mother gone
to the neighbor's. We always liked to find
her at home. We busied ourselves repairing
fences, putting in flood-gates on the river, doing anything to keep away from camp. Miller
himself went back to see Jack within ten days,

remaining a week. None of us stayed at the home ranch any more than we could help. We visited other camps on hatched excuses, until the home round-ups began. When any one else asked us about Jack, we would blow about what a fine claim he had, and what a boost we had given him. When we buckled down to the summer's work the gloom gradually left us. There were men to be sent on the eastern, western, and middle divisions of the general round-up of the Strip. Two men were sent south into the Cheyenne country to catch anything that had winter-drifted. Our range lay in the middle division. Miller and one man looked after it on the general round-up.

It was a busy year with us. Our range was full stocked, and by early fall was rich with fat cattle. We lived with the wagon after the shipping season commenced. Then we missed Jack, although the new cook did the best he knew how. Train after train went out of our pasture, yet the cattle were never missed. We never went to camp now; only the wagon went in after supplies, though we often came within sight of the stabling and corrals in our work.

One day, late in the season, we were getting out a train load of "Barb Wire" cattle,

when who should come toddling along on a
plow nag but Jack himself. Busy as we were,
he held quite a levee, though he did n't give
down much news, nor have anything to say
about himself or the crops. That night at
camp, while the rest of us were arranging the
guards for the night, Miller and Jack prowled
off in an opposite direction from the beef herd,
possibly half a mile, and afoot, too. We
could all see that something was working.
Some trouble was bothering Jack, and he had
come to a friend in need, so we thought.
They did not come back to camp until the
moon was up and the second guard had gone
out to relieve the first. When they came
back not a word was spoken. They unrolled
Miller's bed and slept together.

The next morning as Jack was leaving us
to return to his claim, we overheard him say
to Miller, "I 'll write you." As he faded from
our sight, Miller smiled to himself, as though
he was tickled about something. Finally
Billy Edwards brought things to a head by
asking bluntly, "What 's up with Jack? We
want to know."

"Oh, it 's too good," said Miller. " If that
little game-legged rooster has n't gone and
deluded some girl back in the State into
marrying him, I 'm a horse-thief. You fellows

are all in the play, too. Came here special to see when we could best get away. Wants every one of us to come. He's built another end to his house, double log style, floored both rooms and the middle. Says he will have two fiddlers, and promises us the hog killingest time of our lives. I've accepted the invitation on behalf of the ' J + H 's' without consulting any one."

"But supposing we are busy when it takes place," said Mouse, "then what?"

"But we won't be," answered Miller. "It isn't every day that we have a chance at a wedding in our little family, and when we get the word, this outfit quits then and there. Ordinary callings in life, like cattle matters, must go to the rear until important things are attended to. Every man is expected to don his best togs, and dance to the centre on the word. If it takes a week to turn the trick properly, good enough. Jack and his bride must have a blow-out right. This outfit must do themselves proud. It will be our night to howl, and every man will be a wooly wolf."

We loaded the beeves out the next day, going back after two trains of " Turkey Track " cattle. While we were getting these out, Miller cut out two strays and a cow or two, and sent them to the horse pasture at the home camp. It was getting late in the fall, and we figured that a few more shipments would end it. Miller told the owners to load out what they wanted while the weather was fit, as our saddle horses were getting worn out fast. As we were loading out the last shipment of mixed cattle of our own, the letter came to Miller. Jack would return with his bride on a date only two days off, and the festivities were set for one day later. We pulled into headquarters that night, the first time in six weeks, and turned everything loose. The next morning we overhauled our Sunday bests, and worried around trying to pick out something for a wedding present.

Miller gave the happy pair a little " Flower Pot " cow, which he had rustled in the Cheyenne country on the round-up a few years before. Edwards presented him with a log chain that a bone-picker had lost in our pasture. Mouse gave Jack a four-tined fork which the hay outfit had forgotten when they left. Coon Floyd's compliments went with five cow-bells, which we always thought he rustled from a boomer's wagon that broke down over on the Reno trail. It bothered some of us to rustle something for a present, for you know we couldn't buy anything. We managed to get some deer's antlers, a gray wolf's skin for the bride's tootsies, and several colored sheep-skins, which we had bought from a Mexican horse herd going up the trail that spring. We killed a nice fat little beef, the evening before we started, hanging it out over night to harden. None of the boys knew the brand; in fact, it's bad taste to remember the brand on anything you've beefed. No one troubles himself to notice it carefully. That night a messenger brought a letter to Miller, ordering him to ship out the remnant of "Diamond Tail" cattle as soon as possible. They belonged to a northwest Texas outfit, and we were matur-ing them. The messenger stayed all night, and in the morning asked, " Shall I order cars for you?"

" No, I have a few other things to attend to first," answered Miller.

We took the wagon with us to carry our bedding and the other plunder, driving along with us a cow and a calf of Jack's, the little " Flower Pot " cow, and a beef. Our outfit reached Jack's house by the middle of the afternoon. The first thing was to be intro-duced to the bride. Jack did the honors him-self, presenting each one of us, and seemed just as proud as a little boy with new boots. Then we were given introductions to several good-looking neighbor girls. We began to feel our own inferiority.

While we were hanging up the quarters of beef on some pegs on the north side of the cabin, Edwards said, whispering, "Jack must have pictured this claim mighty hifalutin to that gal, for she's a way up good-looker. Another thing, watch me build to the one inside with the black eyes. I claimed her first, remember. As soon as we get this beef hung up I'm going in and sidle up to her."

"We won't differ with you on that point," remarked Mouse, "but if she takes any special shine to a runt like you, when there's boys like the rest of us standing around, all I've got to say is, her tastes must be a heap sight sorry and depraved. I expect to dance with the bride — in the head set — a whirl or two myself."

"If I'd only thought," chimed in Coon, "I'd sent up to the State and got me a white shirt and a standing collar and a red necktie. You galoots out-hold me on togs. But where I was raised, back down in Palo Pinto County, Texas, I was some punkins as a ladies' man myself — you hear me."

"Oh, you look all right," said Edwards. "You would look all right with only a cotton string around your neck."

After tending to our horses, we all went into the house. There sat Miller talking to the bride just as if he had known her always, with Jack standing with his back to the fire, grinning like a cat eating paste. The neighbor girls fell to getting supper, and our cook turned to and helped. We managed to get fairly well acquainted with the company by the time the meal was over. The fiddlers came early, in fact, dined with us. Jack said if there were enough girls, we could run three sets, and he thought there would be, as he had asked every one both sides of the creek for five miles. The beds were taken down and stowed away, as there would be no use for them that night.

The company came early. Most of the young fellows brought their best girls seated behind them on saddle horses. This manner gave the girl a chance to show her trustful, clinging nature. A horse that would carry double was a prize animal. In settling up a new country, primitive methods crop out as a matter of necessity.

Ben Thorn, an old-timer in the Strip, called off. While the company was gathering, the fiddlers began to tune up, which sent a thrill through us. When Ben gave the word, " Secure your pardners for the first quadrille,"

Miller led out the bride to the first position in the best room, Jack's short leg barring him as a participant. This was the signal for the rest of us, and we fell in promptly. The fiddles struck up "Hounds in the Woods," the prompter's voice rang out "Honors to your pardner," and the dance was on.

Edwards close-herded the black-eyed girl till supper time. Not a one of us got a dance with her even. Mouse admitted next day, as we rode home, that he squeezed her hand several times in the grand right and left, just to show her that she had other admirers, that she need n't throw herself away on any one fellow, but it was no go. After supper Billy corralled her in a corner, she seeming willing, and stuck to her until her brother took her home nigh daylight.

Jack got us boys pardners for every dance. He proved himself clean strain that night, the whitest little Injun on the reservation. We knocked off dancing about midnight and had supper, — good coffee with no end of way-up fine chuck. We ate as we danced, heartily. Supper over, the dance went on full blast. About two o'clock in the morning, the wire edge was well worn off the revelers, and they showed signs of weariness. Miller, noticing it, ordered the Indian war-dance as given by the

Cheyennes. That aroused every one and filled the sets instantly. The fiddlers caught the inspiration and struck into "Sift the Meal and save the Bran." In every grand right and left, we ki-yied as we had witnessed Lo in the dance on festive occasions. At the end of every change, we gave a war-whoop, some of the girls joining in, that would have put to shame any son of the Cheyennes.

It was daybreak when the dance ended and the guests departed. Though we had brought our blankets with us, no one thought of sleeping. Our cook and one of the girls got breakfast. The bride offered to help, but we would n't let her turn her hand. At breakfast we discussed the incidents of the night previous, and we all felt that we had done the occasion justice.

XIII

A QUESTION OF POSSESSION

ALONG in the 8o's there occurred a question of possession in regard to a brand of horses, numbering nearly two hundred head. Courts had figured in former matters, but at this time they were not appealed to, owing to the circumstances. This incident occurred on leased Indian lands unprovided with civil courts, — in a judicial sense, "No-Man's-Land." At this time it seemed that *might* graced the woolsack, while on one side Judge Colt cited his authority, only to be reversed by Judge Parker, breech-loader, short-barreled, a full-choke ten bore. The clash of opinions between these two eminent western authorities was short, determined, and to the point.

A man named Gray had settled in one of the northwest counties in Texas while it was yet the frontier, and by industry and economy of himself and family had established a comfortable home. As a ranchman he had raised the brand of horses in question. The history of this man is somewhat obscured before his coming to Texas. But it was known and admitted that he was a bankrupt, on account of surety debts which he was compelled to pay for friends in his former home in Kentucky. Many a good man had made similar mistakes before him. His neighbors spoke well of him in Texas, and he was looked upon as a good citizen in general.

Ten years of privation and hardship, in their new home, had been met and overcome, and now he could see a ray of hope for the better. The little prosperity which was beginning to dawn upon himself and family met with a sudden shock, in the form of an old judgment, which he always contended his attorneys had paid. In some manner this judgment was revived, transferred to the jurisdiction of his district, and an execution issued against his property. Sheriff Ninde of this county was not as wise as he should have been. When the execution was placed in his hands, he began to look about for property to satisfy the judgment. The exemption laws allowed only a certain number of gentle horses, and as any class of range horses had a cash value then, this brand of horses was levied on to satisfy the judgment.

The range on which these horses were running was at this time an open one, and the sheriff either relied on his reputation as a bad man, or probably did not know any better. The question of possession did not bother him. Still this stock was as liable to range in one county as another. There is one thing quite evident: the sheriff had overlooked the nature of this man Gray, for he was no weakling, inclined to sit down and cry. It was thought that legal advice caused him to take the step he did, and it may be admitted, with no degree of shame, that advice was often given on lines of justice if not of law, in the Lone Star State. There was a time when the decisions of Judge Lynch in that State had the hearty approval of good men. Anyhow, Gray got a few of his friends together, gathered his horses without attracting attention, and within a day's drive crossed into the Indian Territory, where he could defy all the sheriffs in Texas.

When this cold fact first dawned on Sheriff Ninde, he could hardly control himself. With this brand of horses five or six days ahead of him he became worried. The effrontery of any man to deny his authority—the authority of a duly elected sheriff — was a reflection on his record. His bondsmen began to inquire into the situation; in case the property could not be recovered, were they liable as bondsmen? Things looked bad for the sheriff.

The local papers in supporting his candidacy for this office had often spoken of him and his chief deputy as human bloodhounds, — a terror to evil doers. Their election, they maintained, meant a strict enforcement of the laws, and assured the community that a better era would dawn in favor of peace and security of life and property. Ninde was resourceful if anything. He would overtake those horses, overpower the men if necessary, and bring back to his own bailiwick that brand of horse-stock. At least, that was his plan. Of course Gray might object, but that would be a secondary matter. Sheriff Ninde would take time to do this. Having made one mistake, he would make another to right it.

Gray had a brother living in one of the border towns of Kansas, and it was thought he would head for this place. Should he take the horses into the State, all the better, as they could invoke the courts of another State and get other sheriffs to help.

Sixty years of experience with an uncharitable world had made Gray distrustful of his fellow man, though he did not wish to be so. So when he reached his brother in Kansas without molestation, he exercised caution enough to leave the herd of horses in the territory. The courts of this neutral strip were Federal, and located at points in adjoining States, but there was no appeal to them in civil cases. United States marshals looked after the violators of law against the government.

Sheriff Ninde sent his deputy to do the Sherlock act for him as soon as the horses were located. This the deputy had no trouble in doing, as this sized bunch of horses could not well be hidden, nor was there any desire on the part of Gray to conceal them.

The horses were kept under herd day and night in a near-by pasture. Gray usually herded by day, and two young men, one his son, herded by night. Things went on this way for a month. In the mean time the deputy had reported to the sheriff, who came on to personally supervise the undertaking. Gray was on the lookout, and was aware of the deputy's presence. All he could do was to put an extra man on herd at night, arm his men well, and await results.

The deputy secretly engaged seven or eight bad men of the long-haired variety, such as in the early days usually graced the frontier towns with their presence. This brand of human cattle were not the disturbing element on the border line of civilization that writers of that period depicted, nor the authors of the blood-curdling drama portrayed. The average busy citizen paid little attention to them, considering them more ornamental than useful. But this was about the stripe that was wanted and could be secured for the work in hand. A good big bluff was considered sufficient for the end in view. This crowd was mounted, armed to the teeth, and all was ready. Secrecy was enjoined on every one. Led by the sheriff and his deputy, they rode out about midnight to the pasture and found the herd and herders.

"What do you fellows want here?" demanded young Gray, as Ninde and his posse rode up.

"We want these horses," answered the sheriff.

"On what authority?" demanded Gray.

"This is sufficient authority for you," said the sheriff, flashing a six-shooter in young Gray's face. All the heelers to the play now jumped their horses forward, holding their six-shooters over their heads, ratcheting the cylinders of their revolvers by cocking and lowering the hammers, as if nothing but a fight would satisfy their demand for gore.

"If you want these horses that bad," said young Gray, "I reckon you can get them for the present. But I want to tell you one thing — there are sixty head of horses here under herd with ours, outside the '96' brand. They belong to men in town. If you take them out of this pasture to-night, they might consider you a horse-thief and deal with you accordingly. You know you are doing this by force of arms. You have no more authority here than any other man, except what men and guns give you. Good-night, sir, I may see you by daylight."

Calling off his men, they let little grass grow under their feet as they rode to town. The young man roused his father and uncle, who in turn went out and asked their friends to come to their assistance. Together with the owners of the sixty head, by daybreak they had eighteen mounted and armed men.

The sheriff paid no attention to the advice of young Gray, but when day broke he saw that he had more horses than he wanted, as there was a brand or two there he had no claim on, just or unjust, and they must be cut out or trouble would follow. One of the men with Ninde knew of a corral where this work could be done, and to this corral, which was at least fifteen miles from the town where the rescue party of Gray had departed at daybreak, they started. The pursuing posse soon took the trail of the horses from where they left the pasture, and as they headed back toward Texas, it was feared it might take a long, hard ride to overtake them. The gait was now increased to the gallop, not fast, probably covering ten miles an hour, which was considered better time than the herd could make under any circumstances.

After an hour's hard riding, it was evident, from the trail left, that they were not far ahead. The fact that they were carrying off with them horses that were the private property of men in the rescue party did not tend to fortify the sheriff in the good opinion of any of the rescuers. It was now noticed that the herd had left the trail in the direction of a place where there had formerly been a ranch house, the corrals of which were in good repair, as they were frequently used for branding purposes. On coming in sight of these corrals, Gray's party noticed that some kind of work was being carried on, so they approached it cautiously. The word came back that it was the horses.

Gray said to his party, " Keep a short distance behind me. I'll open the ball, if there is any." To the others of his party, it seemed that the supreme moment in the old man's life had come. Over his determined features there spread a smile of the deepest satisfaction, as though some great object in life was about to be accomplished. Yet in that determined look it was evident that he would rather be shot down like a dog than yield to what he felt was tyranny and the denial of his rights. When his party came within a quarter of a mile of the corrals, it was noticed that Ninde and his deputies ceased their work, mounted their horses, and rode out into the open, the sheriff in the lead, and halted to await the meeting.

Gray rode up to within a hundred feet of Ninde's posse, and dismounting handed the reins of his bridle to his son. He advanced with a steady, even stride, a double-barreled shotgun held as though he expected to flush a partridge. At this critical juncture, his party following him up, it seemed that reputations as bad men were due to get action, or suffer a discount at the hands of heretofore peaceable men. Every man in either party had his arms where they would be instantly available should the occasion demand it. When Gray came within easy hailing distance, his challenge was clear and audible to every one. "What in hell are you doing with my horses?"

"I've got to have these horses, sir," answered Ninde.

"Do you realize what it will take to get them?" asked Gray, as he brought his gun, both barrels at full cock, to his shoulder. "Bat an eye, or crook your little finger if you dare, and I'll send your soul glimmering into eternity, if my own goes to hell for it." There was something in the old man's voice that conveyed the impression that these were not idle words. To heed them was the better way, if human life had any value.

"Well, Mr. Gray," said the sheriff, "put down your gun and take your horses. This has been a bad piece of business for us — take your horses and go, sir. My bondsmen can pay that judgment, if they have to."

Gray's son rode around during the conversation, opened the gate, and turned out the horses. One or two men helped him, and the herd was soon on its way to the pasture.

As the men of his party turned to follow Gray, who had remounted, he presented a pitiful sight. His still determined features, relaxed from the high tension to which he had been nerved, were blanched to the color of his hair and beard. It was like a drowning man — with the strength of two — when rescued and brought safely to land, fainting through sheer weakness. A reprieve from death itself or the blood of his fellow man upon his hands had been met and passed. It was some little time before he spoke, then he said: "I reckon it was best, the way things turned out, for I would hate to kill any man, but I would gladly die rather than suffer an injustice or quietly submit to what I felt was a wrong against me."

It was some moments before the party became communicative, as they all had a respect for the old man's feelings. Ninde was on the uneasy seat, for he would not return to the State, though his posse returned somewhat crestfallen. It may be added that the sheriff's bondsmen, upon an examination into the facts in the case, concluded to stand a suit on the developments of some facts which their examination had uncovered in the original proceedings, and the matter was dropped, rather than fight it through in open court.

XIV

THE STORY OF A POKER STEER

HE was born in a chaparral thicket, south of the Nueces River in Texas. It was a warm night in April, with a waning moon hanging like a hunter's horn high overhead, when the subject of this sketch drew his first breath. Ushered into a strange world in the fulfillment of natural laws, he lay trembling on a bed of young grass, listening to the low mooings of his mother as she stood over him in the joy and pride of the first born. But other voices of the night reached his ears; a whippoorwill and his mate were making much ado over the selection of their nesting-place on the border of the thicket. The tantalizing cry of a coyote on the nearest hill caused his mother to turn from him, lifting her head in alarm, and uneasily scenting the night air.

On thus being deserted, and complying with an inborn instinct of fear, he made his first attempt to rise and follow, and although unsuccessful it caused his mother to return and by her gentle nosings and lickings to calm him. Then in an effort to rise he struggled

to his knees, only to collapse like a limp rag.
But after several such attempts he finally stood
on his feet, unsteady on his legs, and tottering
like one drunken. Then his mother nursed
him, and as the new milk warmed his stomach
he gained sufficient assurance of his footing to
wiggle his tail and to butt the feverish caked
udder with his velvety muzzle. After satisfy-
ing his appetite he was loath to lie down and
rest, but must try his legs in toddling around
to investigate this strange world into which he
had been ushered. He smelled of the rich
green leaves of the mesquite, which hung in
festoons about his birth chamber, and trampled
underfoot the grass which carpeted the bower.

After several hours' sleep he was awakened
by a strange twittering above him. The moon
and stars, which were shining so brightly at
the moment of his birth, had grown pale. His
mother was the first to rise, but heedless of
her entreaties he lay still, bewildered by the
increasing light. Animals, however, have
their own ways of teaching their little ones,
and on the dam's first pretense of deserting
him he found his voice, and uttering a plain-
tive cry, struggled to his feet, which caused
his mother to return and comfort him.

Later she enticed him out of the thicket to
enjoy his first sun bath. The warmth seemed

to relieve the stiffness in his joints, and after each nursing during the day he attempted several awkward capers in his fright at a shadow or the rustle of a leaf. Near the middle of the afternoon, his mother being feverish, it was necessary that she should go to the river and slake her thirst. So she enticed him to a place where the grass in former years had grown rank, and as soon as he lay down she cautioned him to be quiet during her enforced absence, and though he was a very young calf he remembered and trusted in her. It was several miles to the river, and she was gone two whole hours, but not once did he disobey. A passing ranchero reined in and rode within three feet of him, but he did not open an eye or even twitch an ear to scare away a fly.

The horseman halted only long enough to notice the flesh-marks. The calf was a dark red except for a white stripe which covered the right side of his face, including his ear and lower jaw, and continued in a narrow band beginning on his withers and broadening as it extended backward until it covered his hips. Aside from his good color the ranchman was pleased with his sex, for a steer those days was better than gold. So the cowman rode away with a pleased expression on his face, but there is a profit and loss account in all things.

When the calf's mother returned she rewarded her offspring for his obedience, and after grazing until dark, she led him into the chaparral thicket and lay down for the night. Thus the first day of his life and a few succeeding ones passed with unvarying monotony. But when he was about a week old his mother allowed him to accompany her to the river, where he met other calves and their dams. She was but a three-year-old, and he was her first baby; so, as they threaded their way through the cattle on the river-bank the little line-back calf was the object of much attention. The other cows were jealous of him, but one old grandmother came up and smelled of him benignantly, as if to say, "Suky, this is a nice baby boy you have here."

Then the young cow, embarrassed by so much attention, crossed the shallow river and went up among some hills where she had once ranged and where the vining mesquite grass grew luxuriantly. There they spent several months, and the calf grew like a weed, and life was one long summer day. He could have lived there always and been content, for he had many pleasures. Other cows, also, brought their calves up to the same place, and he had numerous playmates in his gambols on the hillsides. Among the other calves was a speckled heifer, whose dam was a great crony of his own mother. These two cows were almost inseparable during the entire summer, and it was as natural as the falling of a mesquite bean that he should form a warm attachment for his speckled playmate.

But this June-time of his life had an ending when late in the fall a number of horsemen scoured the hills and drove all the cattle down to the river. It was the first round-up he had ever been in, so he kept very close to his mother's side, and allowed nothing to separate him from her. When the outriders had thrown in all the cattle from the hills and had drifted all those in the river valley together, they moved them back on an open plain and began cutting out. There were many men at the work, and after all the cows and calves had been cut into a separate herd, the other cattle were turned loose. Then with great shoutings the cows were started up the river to a branding-pen several miles distant. Never during his life did the line-back calf forget that day. There was such a rush and hurrah among these horsemen that long before they reached the corrals the line-back's tongue lolled out, for he was now a very fat calf. Only once did he even catch sight of his speckled playmate, **who** was likewise trembling like a fawn.

Inside the corral he rested for a short time in the shade of the palisades. His mother, however, scented with alarm a fire which was being built in the middle of the branding-pen. Several men, who seemed to be the owners, rode through the corralled cows while the cruel irons were being heated. Then the man who directed the work ordered into their saddles a number of swarthy fellows who spoke Spanish, and the work of branding commenced.

The line-back calf kept close to his mother's side, and as long as possible avoided the ropers. But in an unguarded moment the noose of a rope encircled one of his hind feet, and he was thrown upon his side, and in this position the mounted man dragged him up to the fire. His mother followed him closely, but she was afraid of the men, and could only stand at a distance and listen to his piteous crying. The roper, when asked for the brand, replied, "Bar-circle-bar," for that was the brand his mother bore. A tall quiet man who did the branding called to a boy who attended the fire to bring him two irons; with one he stamped the circle, and with the other he made a short horizontal bar on either side of it. Then he took a bloody knife from between his teeth and cut an under-bit from the calf's right ear, inquiring of the owner as he did so, "Do you want this calf left for a bull?"

"No; yearlings will be worth fourteen dollars next spring. He's a first calf — his mother's only a three-year-old."

As he was released he edged away from the fire, forlorn looking. His mother coaxed him over into a corner of the corral, where he dropped exhausted, for with his bleeding ear, his seared side, and a hundred shooting pains in his loins, he felt as if he must surely die. His dam, however, stood over him until the day's work was ended, and kept the other cows from trampling him. When the gates were thrown open and they were given their freedom, he cared nothing for it; he wanted to die. He did not attempt to leave the corral until after darkness had settled over the scene. Then with much persuasion he arose and limped along after his mother. But before he could reach the river, which was at least half a mile away, he sank down exhausted. If he could only slake his terrible thirst he felt he might possibly survive, for the pain had eased somewhat. With every passing breeze of the night he could scent the water, and several times in his feverish fancy he imagined he could hear it as it gurgled over its pebbly bed.

Just at sunrise, ere the heat of the day fell upon him, he struggled to his feet, for he felt it was a matter of life and death with him to reach the river. At last he dragged his pain-racked body down to the rippling water and lowered his head to drink, but it seemed as if every exertion tended to reopen those seared scars, and with the one thing before him that he most desired, he moaned in misery. A little farther away was a deep pool. This he managed to crawl to, and there he remained for a long time, for the water laved his wounds, and he drank and drank. The sun now beat down on him fiercely, and he must seek some shady place for the day, but he started reluctantly to leave, and when he reached the shallows, he turned back to the comfort of the pool and drank again.

A thickety motte of chaparral which grew back from the scattering timber on the river afforded him the shelter and seclusion he wanted, for he dared not trust himself where the grown cattle congregated for the day's siesta. During all his troubles his mother had never forsaken him, and frequently offered him the scanty nourishment of her udder, but he had no appetite and could scarcely raise his eyes to look at her. But time heals all wounds, and within a week he followed his dam back into the hills where grew the succulent grama

grass which he loved. There they remained
for more than a month, and he met his speckled
playmate again.

One day a great flight of birds flew southward, and amidst the cawing of crows and the
croaking of ravens the cattle which ranged
beyond came down out of the hills in long
columns, heading southward. The line-back
calf felt a change himself in the pleasant day's
atmosphere. His mother and the dam of the
speckled calf laid their heads together, and
after scenting the air for several minutes, they
curved their tails — a thing he had never seen
sedate cows do before — and stampeded off
to the south. Of course the line-back calf and
his playmate went along, outrunning their
mothers. They traveled far into the night until
they reached a chaparral thicket, south of the
river, much larger than the one in which he
was born. It was well they sought its shelter,
for two hours before daybreak a norther swept
across the range, which chilled them to the
bone. When day dawned a mist was falling
which incrusted every twig and leaf in crystal
armor.

There were many such northers during the
first winter. The one mysterious thing which
bothered him was, how it was that his mother
could always foretell when one was coming.

But he was glad she could, for she always sought out some cosy place; and now he noticed that his coat had thickened until it was as heavy as the fur on a bear, and he began to feel a contempt for the cold. But springtime came very early in that southern clime, and as he nibbled the first tender blades of grass, he felt an itching in his wintry coat and rubbed off great tufts of hair against the chaparral bushes. Then one night his mother, without a word of farewell, forsook him, and it was several months before he saw her again. But he had the speckled heifer yet for a companion, when suddenly her dam disappeared in the same inexplicable manner as had his own.

He was a yearling now, and with his playmate he ranged up and down the valley of the Nueces for miles. But in June came a heavy rain, almost a deluge, and nearly all the cattle left the valley for the hills, for now there was water everywhere. The two yearlings were the last to go, but one morning while feeding the line-back got a ripe grass burr in his mouth. Then he took warning, for he despised grass burrs, and that evening the two cronies crossed the river and went up into the hills where they had ranged as calves the summer before Within a week, at a lake which both well remembered, they met their mothers face to face.

The steer was on the point of upbraiding his maternal relative for deserting him, when a cream-colored heifer calf came up and nourished itself at the cow's udder. That was too much for him. He understood now why she had left him, and he felt that he was no longer her baby. Piqued with mortification he went to a near-by knoll where the ground was broken, and with his feet pawed up great clouds of dust which settled on his back until the white spot was almost obscured. The next morning he and the speckled heifer went up higher into the hills where the bigger steer cattle ranged. He had not been there the year before, and he had a great curiosity to see what the upper country was like.

In the extreme range of the hills back from the river, the two spent the entire summer, or until the first norther drove them down to the valley. The second winter was much milder than the first one, snow and ice being unknown. So when spring came again they were both very fat, and together they planned — as soon as the June rains came — to go on a little pasear over north on the Frio River. They had met others of their kind from the Frio when out on those hills the summer before, and had found them decently behaved cattle.

But though the outing was feasible and well

planned, it was not to be. For after both had shed their winter coats, the speckled heifer was as pretty a two-year-old as ever roamed the Nueces valley or drank out of its river, and the line-back steer had many rivals. Almost daily he fought other steers of his own age and weight, who were paying altogether too marked attention to his crony. Although he never outwardly upbraided her for it, her coquetry was a matter of no small concern with him. At last one day in April she forced matters to an open rupture between them. A dark red, arch-necked, curly-headed animal came bellowing defiance across their feeding-grounds. Without a moment's hesitation the line-back had accepted the challenge and had locked horns with this Adonis. Though he fought valiantly the battle is ever with the strong, and inch by inch he was forced backward. When he realized that he must yield, he turned to flee, and his rival with one horn caught him behind the fore shoulder, cutting a cruel gash nearly a foot in length. Reaching a point of safety he halted, and as he witnessed his adversary basking in the coquettish, amorous advances of her who had been his constant companion since babyhood, his wrath was uncontrollable. Kneeling, he cut the ground with his horns, throwing up clouds of dust, and then and there he renounced kith and kin, the speckled heifer and the Nueces valley forever. He firmly resolved to start at once for the Frio country. He was a proud two-year-old and had always held his head high. Could his spirit suffer the humiliation of meeting his old companions after such defeat? No! Hurling his bitterest curses on the amorous pair, he turned his face to the northward.

On reaching the Nueces, feverish in anger, he drank sparingly, kneeling against the soft river's bank, cutting it with his horns, and matting his forehead with red mud. It was a momentous day in his life. He distinctly remembered the physical pain he had suffered once in a branding-pen, but that was nothing compared to this. Surely his years had been few and full of trouble. He hardly knew which way to turn. Finally he concluded to lie down on a knoll and rest until nightfall, when he would start on his journey to the Frio. Just how he was to reach that country troubled him. He was a cautious fellow; he knew he must have water on the way, and the rains had not yet fallen.

Near the middle of the afternoon an incident occurred which changed the whole course of his after-life. From his position on the knoll he witnessed the approach of four horsemen who apparently were bent on driving all the cattle in that vicinity out of their way. To get a better view he arose, for it was evident they had no intention of disturbing him. When they had drifted away all the cattle for a mile on both sides of the river, one of the horsemen rode back and signaled to some one in the distance. Then the line-back steer saw something new, for coming over the brow of the hill was a great column of cattle. He had never witnessed such a procession of his kind before. When the leaders had reached the river, the rear was just coming over the brow of the hill, for the column was fully a mile in length. The line-back steer classed them as strangers, probably bound for the Frio, for that was the remotest country in his knowledge. As he slowly approached the herd, which was then crowding into the river, he noticed that they were nearly all two-year-olds like himself. Why not accompany them? His resolution to leave the Nueces valley was still uppermost in his mind. But when he attempted to join in, a dark-skinned man on a horse chased him away, cursing him in Spanish as he ran. Then he thought they must be exclusive, and wondered where they came from.

But when the line-back steer once resolved to do anything, the determination became a consuming desire. He threw the very intensity of his existence into his resolution of the morning. He would leave the Nueces valley with those cattle — or alone, it mattered not. So after they had watered and grazed out from the river, he followed at a respectful distance. Once again he tried to enter the herd, but an outrider cut him off. The man was well mounted, and running his horse up to him he took up his tail, wrapped the brush around the pommel of his saddle, and by a dexterous turn of his horse threw him until he spun like a top. The horseman laughed. The ground was sandy, and while the throwing frightened him, never for an instant did it shake his determination.

So after darkness had fallen and the men had bedded their cattle for the night, he slipped through the guard on night-herd and lay down among the others. He complimented himself on his craftiness, but never dreamed that this was a trail herd, bound for some other country three hundred miles beyond his native Texas. The company was congenial; it numbered thirty-five hundred two-year-old steers like himself, and strangely no one ever noticed him until long after they had crossed the Frio. Then a swing man one day called his foreman's attention to a stray, line-backed, bar-circle-bar steer in the herd. The foreman only gave him a passing glance, saying, "Let him alone; we may get a jug of whiskey for him if some trail cutter don't claim him before we cross Red River."

Now Red River was the northern boundary of his native State, and though he was unconscious of his destination, he was delighted with his new life and its constant change of scene. He also rejoiced that every hour carried him farther and farther from the Nueces valley, where he had suffered so much physical pain and humiliation. So for several months he traveled northward with the herd. He swam rivers and grazed in contentment across flowery prairies, mesas and broken country. Yet it mattered nothing to him where he was going, for his every need was satisfied. These men with the herd were friendly to him, for they anticipated his wants by choosing the best grazing, so arranging matters that he reached water daily, and selecting a dry bed ground for him at night. And when strange copper-colored men with feathers in their hair rode along beside the herd he felt no fear.

The provincial ideas of his youth underwent a complete change within the first month of

trail life. When he swam Red River with the
leaders of the herd, he not only bade farewell
to his native soil, but burned all bridges behind
him. To the line-back steer, existence on the
Nueces had been very simple. But now his
views were broadening. Was not he a unit of
millions of his kind, all forging forward like
brigades of a king's army to possess themselves of some unconquered country? These
men with whom he was associated were the
vikings of the Plain. The Red Man was conquered, and, daily, the skulls of the buffalo, his
predecessors, stared vacantly into his face.

By the middle of summer they reached their
destination, for the cattle were contracted to a
cowman in the Cherokee Strip, Indian Territory. The day of delivery had arrived. The
herd was driven into a pasture where they met
another outfit of horsemen similar to their own.
The cattle were strung out and counted. The
men agreed on the numbers. But watchful
eyes scanned every brand as they passed in
review, and the men in the receiving outfit
called the attention of their employer to the
fact that there were several strays in the herd
not in the road brand. One of these strays was
a line-back, bar-circle-bar, two-year-old steer.
There were also others; when fifteen of them
had been cut out and the buyer asked the trail

foreman if he was willing to include them in the bill of sale, the latter smilingly replied: "Not on your life, Captain. You can't keep them out of a herd. Down in my country we call strays like them *poker steers.*"

And so there were turned loose in the Cold-water Pool, one of the large pastures in the Strip, fifteen strays. That night, in a dug-out on that range, the home outfit of cowboys played poker until nearly morning. There were seven men in the camp entitled to share in this flotsam on their range, the extra steer falling to the foreman. Mentally they had a list of the brands, and before the game opened the strays were divided among the participants. An animal was represented by ten beans. At the beginning the boys played cautiously, counting every card at its true worth in a hazard of chance. But as the game wore on and the more fortunate ones saw their chips increase, the weaker ones were gradually forced out. At midnight but five players remained in the game. By three in the morning the foreman lost his last bean, and ordered the men into their blankets, saying they must be in their saddles by dawn, riding the fences, scattering and locating the new cattle. As the men yawningly arose to obey, Dick Larkin defiantly said to the winners, " I've just got ten beans left, and I'll cut high card with any man to see who takes mine or I take one of his poker steers."

"My father was killed in the battle of the Wilderness," replied Tex, "and I'm as game a breed as you are. I'll match your beans and pit you my bar-circle-bar steer."

"My sire was born in Ireland and is living yet," retorted Bold Richard. "Cut the cards, young fellow."

"The proposition is yours — cut first yourself."

The other players languidly returned to the table. Larkin cut a five spot of clubs and was in the act of tearing it in two, when Tex turned the tray of spades. Thus, on the turn of a low card, the line-back steer passed into the questionable possession of Dick Larkin. The Cherokee Strip wrought magic in a Texas steer. One or two winters in its rigorous climate transformed the gaunt long-horn into a marketable beef. The line-back steer met the rigors of the first winter and by June was as glossy as a gentleman's silk tile. But at that spring round-up there was a special inspector from Texas, and no sooner did his eye fall upon the bar-circle-bar steer than he opened his book and showed the brand and his authority to claim him. When Dick Larkin asked to see his credentials, the inspector not only produced them, but gave the owner's name and the county in which the brand was a matter of record. There was no going back on that, and the Texas man took the line-back steer. But the round-up stayed all night in the Pool pasture, and Larkin made it his business to get on second guard in night-herding the cut. He had previously assisted in bedding down the cattle for the night, and made it a point to see that the poker three-year-old lay down on the outer edge of the bed ground. The next morning the line-back steer was on his chosen range in the south end of the pasture. How he escaped was never known; there are ways and ways in a cow country.

At daybreak the round-up moved into the next pasture, the wagons, cut and saddle horses following. The special inspector was kept so busy for the next week that he never had time to look over the winter drift and strays, which now numbered nearly two thousand cattle. When the work ended the inspector missed the line-back steer. He said nothing, however, but exercised caution enough to take what cattle he had gathered up into Kansas for pasturage.

When the men who had gone that year on the round-up on the western division returned,

there was a man from Reece's camp in the
Strip, east on Black Bear, who asked permis-
sion to leave about a dozen cattle in the Pool.
He was alone, and, saying he would bring another man with him during the shipping season, he went his way. But when Reece's men
came back after their winter drift during the
beef-gathering season, Bold Richard Larkin
bantered the one who had left the cattle for a
poker game, pitting the line-back three-year-
old against a white poker cow then in the Pool
pasture and belonging to the man from Black
Bear. It was a short but spirited game. At its
end the bar-circle-bar steer went home with
Reece's man. There was a protective code
of honor among rustlers, and Larkin gave the
new owner the history of the steer. He told
him that the brand was of record in McMullen
County, Texas, warned him of special inspectors, and gave him other necessary information.

The men from the Coldwater Pool, who
went on the eastern division of the round-up
next spring, came back and reported having
seen a certain line-back poker steer, but the
bar-circle-bar had somehow changed, until
now it was known as the *pilot wheel*. And, so
report came back, in the three weeks' work
that spring, the line-back pilot-wheel steer had

changed owners no less than five times. Late
that fall word came down from Fant's pasture
up west on the Salt Fork to send a man or two
up there, as Coldwater Pool cattle had been
seen on that range. Larkin and another lad
went up to a beef round-up, and almost the
first steer Bold Richard laid his eyes on was
an under-bit, line-back, once a bar-circle-bar
but now a pilot-wheel beef. Larkin swore
by all the saints he would know that steer in
Hades. Then Abner Taylor called Bold Richard aside and told him that he had won the
steer about a week before from an Eagle
Chief man, who had also won the beef from
another man east on Black Bear during the
spring round-up. The explanation satisfied
Larkin, who recognized the existing code
among rustlers.

The next spring the line-back steer was a
five-year-old. Three winters in that northern
climate had put the finishing touches on him.
He was a beauty. But Abner Taylor knew he
dared not ship him to a market, for there
he would have to run a regular gauntlet of
inspectors. There was another chance open,
however. Fant, Taylor's employer, had many
Indian contracts. One contract in particular
required three thousand northern wintered
cattle for the Fort Peck Indian Reservation

in northeast Montana. Fant had wintered the cattle with which to fill this contract on his Salt Fork range in the Cherokee Strip. When the cowman cast about for a foreman on starting the herd for Fort Peck, the fact that Abner Taylor was a Texan was sufficient recommendation with Fant. And the line-back beef and several other poker steers went along.

The wintered herd of beeves were grazed across to Fort Peck in little less than three months. On reaching the agency, the cattle were in fine condition and ready to issue to the Indian wards of our Christian nation. In the very first allotment from this herd the line-back beef was cut off with thirty others. It was fitting that he should die in his prime. As the thirty head were let out of the agency corral, a great shouting arose among the braves who were to make the kill. A murderous fire from a hundred repeaters was poured into the running cattle. Several fell to their knees, then rose and struggled on. The scene was worthy of savages. As the cattle scattered several Indians singled out the line-back poker steer. One specially well-mounted brave ran his pony along beside him and pumped the contents of his carbine into the beef's side. With the blood frothing from his nostrils, the line-back turned and catching the horse with his horn disemboweled him. The Indian had thrown himself on the side of his mount to avoid the sudden thrust, and, as the pony fell, he was pinned under him. With admirable tenacity of life the pilot-wheel steer staggered back and made several efforts to gore the dying horse and helpless rider, but with a dozen shots through his vitals, he sank down and expired. A destiny, over which he had no seeming control, willed that he should yield to the grim reaper nearly three thousand miles from his birthplace on the sunny Nueces.

Abner Taylor, witnessing the incident, rode over to a companion and inquired: "Did you notice my line-back poker steer play his last trump? From the bottom of my heart I wish he had killed the Indian instead of the pony."

051088